Southern Exposure

A play in two acts

By

Claude Brickell

United States Copyright
PAu 3-458-732
June 5, 2008
by author
ISBN: 9798827105473

BricBooks
Publishing

For my mother
who opened the world of theater to me

and for Director Mark Rydell
of the Actors Studio West
where the play was developed, and who personally nurtured me with it

Place: A small town in the South

Time: Late October, present

Characters

ABRAHAM: amiable black man of many years and the estate's caretaker

LAURIE: plain woman in her thirties and caregiver to Bettye Lynn

CHARLENE: likable woman of Angela's age and a next door neighbor

BETTYE LYNN BATEMAN: strong-willed woman of several years with more energy than a mad bull and the play's central character

ANGELA BATEMAN: attractive, graceful woman twenty years her mother's junior and Hollywood film and TV star with a determined agenda

MARGE BATEMAN: plump yet pretty woman two-years younger than her sister Angela

RAWLEY BATEMAN: thin, mildly attractive and polite in the southern tradition, five years younger than his sister Marge

MR. RIVENBARK *(rhy-vin-bark)*: short, portly and amiable elderly man and an attorney by profession

Synopsis at end
as well as royalty guidelines

Act One

Scene One

The scene is the wide front porch of a large old house in a small town somewhere in the Deep South with huge Ionic columns soaring upward in the Greek revival tradition. There is a cane table with chairs near one end of the porch, the one possibly closest to the apron. At the other end is a wooden wheelchair ramp that leads down to the front yard, now strewn with fallen leaves. A walkway, off to one side, leads, presumably, down to the street.

At curtain's rise, ABRAHAM, an amiable black man of many years, wearing old trousers and a wool plaid shirt, is raking up leaves in the yard. He is the handyman who lives out back on the property. He is not retarded but he is somewhat slow and he is humming an old tune as he performs his task. The time is mid-morning.

The screen door opens, presently, and, LAURIE, a plane woman in her thirties, comes out. She is wearing a light sweater and cotton dress that might easily double as a nurse, and, in fact, she is a hired caregiver. She then sits down on the steps where she begins observing Abraham at work. After a moment, she rubs her arms to warm them up.

LAURIE
It's gettin' kinda cold out here, Abraham.

ABRAHAM
Yes, ma'am, it sho is. It sho'nuf is. And it's gonna git real cold t'night, too. I heard that on the radio. Those lil' chillins is gonna have to wrap up real good, I figure, when they comes out t'night.

LAURIE
Oh, that's right; tonight's Halloween, isn't it?

ABRAHAM

Yes, ma'am, it sho is.

Abraham then goes over to the side of the porch and brings back an apple basket in which to hold his raked leaves.

ABRAHAM (Cont'd)

Ain't seen Miss Angela out, yet.

LAURIE

Well, I know she must be exhausted from her trip, comin' all the way here from way out in California. That's a long way to come.

ABRAHAM

Yes, ma'am, it sho is. That's a *long* way.

LAURIE

I just can't wait to meet her. I've always thought she was so pretty.

ABRAHAM

Yes, ma'am, she sho is. She is very pretty.

LAURIE

I remember her in 'Long Into The Night.' She was just beautiful, then. I loved that movie. Did you ever see that, Abraham?

ABRAHAM

No, ma'am, I did not. I don't get to the picture show much. But I seen one of her movies, once.

LAURIE

Which one was that?

ABRAHAM
(stopping his raking)
Well, let me see, now. Let me see. I believe it was called 'Heaven' and somethin'.

LAURIE
'If Heaven Only Knew.' Yes, that was so wonderful. What does she look like, now? I bet she's every bit as pretty as she was, then.

ABRAHAM
(resuming his work)
Yes, ma'am, she sho is. She sho is. She is ever bit as pretty. 'Course, I ain't seen her when she come in last night. But, I seen her 'bout three years ago when she was here and she was awful pretty, then.

LAURIE
(looking up at the trees)
I think you have your work cut out for you, Abraham. Looks like all those red and gold leaves up there are 'bout ready to come down any minute, now.

ABRAHAM
(chuckling)
Sho'nuf, Miss Laurie. Sho'nuf. And, I am *ready* for 'em.

LAURIE
(looking out at the yard)
It's so peaceful and quiet, out here.

ABRAHAM
Yes, ma'am, it sho is. But, it ain't gonna be fo'long. Not after Miss Bettye comes out. Oh, no! It won't be peaceful, then. No, ma'am! It won't be peaceful, then.

LAURIE
She's takin' her mornin' bath, right now, so, I thought I'd sneak myself a short break.

ABRAHAM
(chuckling, again)
That's a good time fo'it, Miss Laurie. But, y'all won't have long. No, ma'am. Y'all won't have long, at all. I 'specs the paper'll be comin' any minute, now, and y'all knows how Miss Bettye waits fo'her paper. She'll be callin' fo'that, in no time. She gots to have her puzzle, ever mornin'.

LAURIE
What's gonna happen to you, Abraham, after all this? I mean after they take Mrs. Bateman away. What's gonna happen to you, then?

ABRAHAM
(shaking his head)
Oh, Miss Laurie, I don't know. I just do not know.

LAURIE
You have family, somewhere?

ABRAHAM
No, ma'am, 'cept my cousin Nathanial up in Ulm *(ull-em)*. That's all in the world I gots.

LAURIE
You've lived here a long time, haven't you?

ABRAHAM
Sho'nuf. I have lived here a *long* time. Ever since I was nineteen years old. I didn't have no where else to go, y'all sees. Mama worked for the Batemans back then and always had. And when I
(Cont'd)

ABRAHAM (Cont'd)
comes home after the war… well, I couldn't rightly take care of myself. So, when mama died, Judge Bateman, he come to me and he said, 'Abe,' he said, 'y'alls gonna come live right out back of us in this here shed and we a'gonna see y'all is taken good care of.

LAURIE
You were wounded in the war, Abraham?

ABRAHAM
Well, Miss Laurie, not exactly. Not physically.
(pausing in thought)

LAURIE
You'd prefer not to talk about it…?

ABRAHAM
Well, Miss Laurie… I was in a terrible shock when I comes home, y'all sees. A terrible shock 'cause I had witnessed a terrible thing and I just couldn't get over it. I still got the shakes 'bout it most of the time.

LAURIE
My word! What happened? I mean…

ABRAHAM
Well, Miss Laurie, I don't talk much about it. *(sighing)* I was… I was, well… the only one in my platoon that survived. They was all wiped out one night, right before my eyes.

LAURIE
Oh, that's awful, Abraham. Was it a bomb?

ABRAHAM

No, Miss Laurie. *(sighing, again)* They was wiped out by our own men comin' up from behind. 'Cept, we was all black and they was all white. And, later on, they just went and covered it all up. They just kept on tellin' me, over and over in the mental ward, that it ain't never happened. But, they was lyin'. It *did* happen. It sho 'nuf did.

LAURIE

That's just terrible!

ABRAHAM
(noticeably shaken)
I know, Miss Laurie. I know. I sho do know that.

Abraham pauses, again, to get hold of himself.

ABRAHAM (Cont'd)
So, after mama died, I comes here to live and I have been here ever since.

LAURIE
Well, I'm sure it was all for the best.

ABRAHAM
Oh, yes, ma'am. It sho was. It *sho* was. I don't know what would've happened to me seein' as I'm not too awful smart, and all.

LAURIE
Well, I think you are. A lot more than most of 'em 'round here suspect.

ABRAHAM
I don't know 'bout that, Miss Laurie. Could be. Could be.

A second woman, CHARLENE, comes up the front walk toward the house. She is the same age as Angela and wears a cardigan over her cotton dress. And she is carrying a large bowl in one hand and a smaller one in the other.

CHARLENE
Mornin,' Abraham!

ABRAHAM
(turning)
Mornin,' Miss Charlene. Y'all comin' over fo'a visit?

CHARLENE
I brought over some of Franklin's sweet potatoes from his garden to give to Mrs. Bateman. We had so many this year, why, they're just rottin' out in the shed.
(noticing Laurie)
And you must be Laurie.

Laurie has stood up to greet Charlene as she is approaching the porch steps.

LAURIE
Yes, ma'am, I am.

CHARLENE
Well, that's just precious. I'm Charlene Meeks. We're the neighbors in the house next door.

LAURIE
Oh! Nice to meet you.

CHARLENE
Well, it's nice to meet you, too. I've heard all about how wonderful you've been for Mrs. Bateman.

LAURIE
I wish I could've been here longer. But, at least I got to meet you on my last day here.

CHARLENE
Your last *day*! You haven't been here a full week, yet! Has Mrs. Bateman gone and let you go, already?

LAURIE
Oh, no, ma'am. But, seein' as they're takin' Mrs. Bateman away for good, this afternoon, they won't be needin' me here, any longer.

Charlene looks around to Abraham.

CHARLENE
Abraham? Are they takin' Mrs. Bateman away?

Abraham scratches his head not wanting to get too involved.

ABRAHAM
Well, Miss Charlene, that's what I been told. That is sho what I have been told.

CHARLENE
My livin' days. I had no *idea*! Does Mrs. Bateman know this, yet?

LAURIE
I don't think so. They was kinda waitin' for her daughter to tell her 'bout it, first.

CHARLENE
Where *is* Angela?

LAURIE

She hasn't come down, yet. I can't wait to meet her. I've never met a real live movie star, before.

CHARLENE

Well, I just never.
(looking down at her bowls)
And, here, I brought all these sweet potatoes over for supper, tonight, and my candied apples for the trick-o'-treaters, later on.

LAURIE

You want me to take those inside for you, Mrs. Meeks?

CHARLENE

Oh, no, hun, I'll take 'em in, myself.
(looking around at Abraham, again)
How long have ya'all known, Abraham... 'bout Mrs. Bateman, I mean?

ABRAHAM

(scratching his head, again)
Well, Miss Charlene, Mr. Gershwin, the lawyer, he done told me yesterdy mornin'. That's when I knowed. That is when I knowed. Mr. Gershwin, he said Miss Angela was comin' here on the plane and that Miss Bettye was goin' away to the old folks home.

CHARLENE

The *old* folks home!

LAURIE

He means The Good Shepherd Retirement Home up in Arkadelphia. That's where they're takin' Mrs. Bateman. Well, that's what I've been told, anyway.

There is a suddenly commotion going on, within.

MRS. BATEMAN (OS)

I don't want my sweater! Take that away! I want my shawl! Where's my shawl? That's right. Here, give it to me! Where's Laurie? *Laurie!* Will *somebody* wheel me out to the porch! *Laurie*! Where is *Laurie*?

LAURIE

I'm comin,' Mrs. Bateman! Excuse me, Mrs. Meeks.

Laurie turns and hurries back through the screen door into the house.

CHARLENE
(turning)
Abraham!
(descending, in haste, back down)
Just what all did Mr. Gershwin tell you, yesterdy?

ABRAHAM
(stopping his work, again)
'Bout Miss Bettye, Miss Charlene?

CHARLENE

Yes! What all did he say?

ABRAHAM

Well, Miss Charlene, he didn't say much mo' than that. Not much mo' than that. Just that he was sendin' a big car 'round to pick Miss Bettye up at fo' p.m. t'day. That's what he done told me.

CHARLENE

Four *p.m.*! And that's all right with Angela?

ABRAHAM
Well, I don't know 'bout that, Miss Charlene. I ain't seen Miss Angela, yet. She come in late last night and she ain't been down here, yet. But, I 'specs she knows.

CHARLENE
And what about Marge? Does she know anything about this?

ABRAHAM
Well, I don't know 'bout that, Miss Charlene. Just Miss Angela's all that's here, right now.

CHARLENE
Well, I feel just *awful*.

ABRAHAM
Yes, Miss Charlene. I feels awful, too. I feels real bad.

Charlene looks back up at the house.

CHARLENE
It's not gonna be the same 'round here without Mrs. Bateman. This place'll be just dreadful. I've lived my whole life right next door to this big old house and I've never known it to be any other way. Why, I can still see my mother and all the other Magnolia ladies playin' bridge right up there on the porch, at least a hundred times or more. 'Course, that was years ago. *(sighing)* I just can't imagine it.

ABRAHAM
They's gonna be sellin' the house, too, Miss Charlene.

CHARLENE
(turning back to him)
Sellin' it!

ABRAHAM
Yes, ma'am. They sho is. They sho is. That is what Mr. Gershwin done told me, yesterdy. And, I have t'move on somewheres else, myself. He done told me that, too.

CHARLENE
Oh, Abraham, I'm *so* sorry! I never thought about that. Where in the world will you go?

ABRAHAM
I don't knows, Miss Charlene. I do not knows.

CHARLENE
Well, don't you worry 'bout a thing. Franklin and I will see to it you have a place to go to, cross my heart, now.
(looking back up at the house)
My head is just swimmin'. Things are beginnin' to happen' just too fast 'round here for my likin'.

ABRAHAM
Yes, Miss Charlene, they's sho is. They's happenin' real fast.

More commotion within.

MRS. BATEMAN (OS)
Watch out for my Duncan Phyfe table, there. You nearly clipped it. And keep away from that rosewood chair, ya hear? That was my mother's! Now, come on, wheel me on out to the porch! Calley! Where's my coffee? I want my coffee out on the porch, ya hear?!

The screen door flies open as Laurie is wheeling Mrs. Bateman out in a vintage wheelchair. BETTYE LYNN BATEMAN is a woman of several years but she's got more energy than a mad bull. She holds a cane in one hand wielding it like a saber wherever she goes. In fact, it is her cane that pushes the screen door open as she comes rolling out. She is wearing a long sleeve dress with a crocheted shawl over her shoulders.

LAURIE
Calley's bringin' your coffee out with your breakfast, Mrs. Bateman.

MRS. BATEMAN
I told you I don't *want* breakfast!

LAURIE
You don't want *breakfast*! I thought you always had your breakfast out here on the porch.

MRS. BATEMAN
I said I don't want *breakfast*! Are you deaf, girl? I want my coffee and I want nothin' else, ya hear?

CHARLENE
(from yard)
Good mornin,' Mrs. Bateman.

MRS. BATEMAN
What's good about it, Charlene? And how's your mother?

CHARLENE
Oh, she's just fine.

MRS. BATEMAN
Well, you tell her Bettye Lynn's gonna be over to see her one of these days, just as soon as I get my strength back, ya hear?

CHARLENE
Right, Mrs. Bateman. I will tell her.

MRS. BATEMAN

Us agein' folks have to look out for each other, these days. No tellin' what's bein' pulled on us right under our very noses.

Charlene is then climbing back up the steps.

CHARLENE

Oh, now, Mrs. Bateman. Nobody's gonna pull anything on my mother while I'm around.

MRS. BATEMAN

Well, she is lucky, then. Can't say the same for things over here. I got a hunch somebody's plottin' somethin' against me. I'm just not sure what it is, yet. What you got there?

CHARLENE

I brought over some of Franklin's homegrown sweet potatoes. They're just delicious. I thought you might like to have some for supper, tonight.

MRS. BATEMAN

That's right nice of you, Charlene. I surely would.

CHARLENE

And, this here's some of my candied apples. You know, the little bitty baby ones I coat every year for the kids on Halloween?

MRS. BATEMAN

Hallo*ween*!

CHARLENE

Why, yes. Holloween's tonight.

MRS. BATEMAN
(looking around at all)
I didn't know Halloween was *tonight*! Nobody 'round here ever tells me a damn thing. I might as well be nothin' but a *stone* stoop. Abraham!

ABRAHAM
(approaching porch)
Yes, Miss Bettye. I am right here.

MRS. BATEMAN
Where is my jack-o'-lantern? You know I always have a jack-o'-lantern, every Halloween, right here on the edge of the porch so all the kids can see it when they come up the walk. Now, where is it?

ABRAHAM
(scratching his head)
Well, I just didn't think ya'll'd...

MRS. BATEMAN
You go right down to Mr. Jameson's grocery store, this minute, and you tell him Mrs. Bateman sent you down to pick out one of his pumpkins, ya here?

ABRAHAM
Yes, ma'am.

MRS. BATEMAN
And you get a nice round one. Don't let him send one of those lopsided ones like he did, last year. I want a nice round one like I always have, ya hear?

ABRAHAM
Yes, ma'am. I sho will.

MRS. BATEMAN

And when you get back here, you take it 'round to Calley in the kitchen and she'll carve it out like she always does, ya hear me?

ABRAHAM

Yes, ma'am. I will do that, too.

MRS. BATEMAN

We got to have a jack-o'-lantern to scare all the witches and the goblins away. Isn't that right, Charlene?

CHARLENE

Oh, yes, Mrs. Bateman. It surely is.

ABRAHAM
(more serious, than not)

Oh, Miss Bettye, don't say such a thing. We don't need no witches and no goblins.

MRS. BATEMAN

Well, it may be too late for that. We've already got one witch and she's upstairs, as we speak. But if we're lucky, we can still scare a few of those goblins away.

ABRAHAM

I am goin' right now, Miss Bettye. Right now.

Abraham starts off for the side of the house.

MRS. BATEMAN
(glancing down to the street)

Wait a minute! I think I see Joe Bob, Jr. comin' up Poplar Street right this very minute with my mornin' paper. Go down and get my mornin' paper 'fore you go off to the grocery store. I've got to have my paper.

ABRAHAM
Yes, ma'am. I sho will. I sho will.

Abraham drops his leaf broom against the porch and hurries off down the walk toward the street, disappearing offstage.

MRS. BATEMAN
Where in the hell is my *coffee*?! Laurie, go back inside and bring out my coffee right this minute, ya hear? It'll be stone cold 'fore I even get to take my first sip.

LAURIE
Yes, Mrs. Bateman. I'll go right this instant.

MRS. BATEMAN
Wait just a minute! Wheel me over to the table, first.

LAURIE
Of course, Mrs. Bateman.
         (Laurie then pushes the wheelchair over)
We'll just get you parked right up here at the table… and then I'll go get your coffee.

After wheeling to the table, Laurie then turns and disappears through the screen door, again. Charlene then moves to the table, placing the two bowls down on it, then sits down in one of the chairs.

CHARLENE
Is everything all right over here, Mrs. Bateman?

MRS. BATEMAN
Hell, no! What's there to be right? My arthritis is acting up, again, just like it always does every time there's a change in the weather. I might as well be a walking barometer. Scratch that, Charlene. A *rollin'* one's more like it.

CHARLENE

Well, I mean... Well...

MRS. BATEMAN

Go on, now, say what you mean. Cat's always had your tongue ever since you were knee-high to a hitchin' post. Go on, say what you mean!

CHARLENE

Well, you are very dear to us, Mrs. Bateman, you know that. You were always my mother's dearest friend.

MRS. BATEMAN

I know that and, still am.
(looking out and sighing)
All I know is that daughter of mine flew in here last night—much to my surprise—and I figure she must be cookin' somethin' up. I'm just not sure what it is.

CHARLENE

You haven't talked to her, yet?

MRS. BATEMAN

No, I have not, and I'm not sure I want to.

CHARLENE

Well, if you need anything, you will let us know, won't you? I mean if we can do anything to help, Franklin and I... well...

MRS. BATEMAN

You could bring over a shotgun. I could use one 'bout now.

CHARLENE

Oh, Mrs. Bateman. Don't say such a thing.

MRS. BATEMAN
I'm jokin,' Charlene. 'Course, that's all one sees on TV these days. Everybody blowin' the heads off of everbody else. I figure I'm due a few good shots of my own.
(chuckling to herself)

Laurie comes out the screen door, again, with a mug of hot coffee, in hand.

LAURIE
Here's your coffee, Mrs. Bateman, just like you like it. Steamin' hot.

Laurie then places the mug down before Mrs. Bateman and the woman then picks it up and begins blowing air into the steam to cool it off. Afterwards, she takes a sip.

LAURIE (Cont'd)
Would you like some, too, Mrs. Meeks?

CHARLENE
Oh, no, thank you, Laurie. I'm not gonna be here, that long. I've got a coconut cake in the oven I've got to get back to. But, thank you, all the same.

Abraham comes hurriedly up the walk with the morning paper.

ABRAHAM
Here's y'alls paper, Miss Bettye. I gots it right here. Right here.

Abraham then leaps up the steps, placing the paper down on the table for Mrs. Bateman.

MRS. BATEMAN
Thank you, Abraham. I don't know what in the world I'd do without you. You are the only one around here I can ever depend on.

ABRAHAM
Sho'nuf, Miss Bettye. Sho'nuf. Ya'lls can always depend on me.

MRS. BATEMAN
Did you tell Laurie how long you've been with us?

LAURIE
Yes, Mrs. Bateman, he did. He said, ever since he was nineteen.

ABRAHAM
Yes, ma'am, that is the honest truth. Ever since I was nineteen years old.

MRS. BATEMAN
And, did you tell her your name, too?

LAURIE
Oh, yes, he did. It's Abraham. That's a fine Biblical name, too.

MRS. BATEMAN
That's not the whole of it. Go on, Abraham. Tell her your *full* name.

ABRAHAM
Well, my name is Abraham Lincoln George Washington Lee.

LAURIE
(her mouth dropping open)
Oh, my word! Is that true?

ABRAHAM
Yes, ma'am. That is my name. That is sho my name. That is the name my mama done give me. Abraham Lincoln George Washington Lee.

MRS. BATEMAN
Did you ever hear a name like that, Laurie?

LAURIE
Never! Why, I'm just astounded.

MRS. BATEMAN
(back to Abraham)
Now, hurry on down to Mr. Jameson's store, ya hear?

ABRAHAM
Yes, ma'am, Miss Bettye. I am goin'. I am goin', right now!

Abraham hurries back down the steps then disappears around the back of the house.

MRS. BATEMAN
We should all be as humble as Abraham. The Lord would be right pleased about that, wouldn't he, Charlene?

CHARLENE
Right, Mrs. Bateman. He surely would.
(standing up, reaching for the bowls, again)
Well, I'll just take these on back to Calley in the kitchen.

Laurie then goes to open the screen door for her, then Charlene disappears, inside. Mrs. Bateman then reaches into her side basket, pulling out her glasses and putting them on. Then, she takes out her pencil and reaches for the newspaper, as well.

MRS. BATEMAN
Let's see, now, what tricks they've got in the puzzle, today.
Seein's how it's Halloween, there's no tellin' what they've got up
their sleeves.

Mrs. Bateman then opens the paper, locating the puzzle.

LAURIE
Are you excited 'bout seein' your daughter, this mornin', Mrs.
Bateman?

MRS. BATEMAN
(scanning puzzle clues)
'Bout as excited as an old cat caught out in the rain.

LAURIE
You must be very proud to have a daughter who's an actress.

MRS. BATEMAN
(ignoring the question)
Five letter word for 'sorceress.' *Ha*! 'W-i-t-c-h.'

LAURIE
I used to dream of bein' an actress, myself, when I was young.

MRS. BATEMAN
Nothin' wrong with what you do now, Laurie. A caregiver's a
right noble profession.

LAURIE
Oh, I know that, Mrs. Bateman. I love helpin' elderly people out,
and all that. I can't think of anything else I'd rather be doin.' But,
I just can't imagine what it must be like bein' a real *actress*. And,
a *movie* star, too. Well, I just can't imagine it.

                    MRS. BATEMAN
Then, don't even try.

Mrs. Bateman then sips more of her coffee.

                    ANGELA (OS)
Where's my mother, Calley? Is she outside on the porch?

Laurie turns, excitedly, toward the screen door.

                    LAURIE
Oh, I think I hear Miss Bateman, now. She's comin' out here, right now. Oh, Mrs. Bateman, my heart is just poundin.' I am in a tether.

                    MRS. BATEMAN
Well, don't you go and have a seizure over it.

The screen door opens and ANGELA BATEMAN comes out. She is still an attractive woman in her age, wearing a tailored winter suit, and is quite graceful. She carries a movie script and a cell phone, in hand. Mrs. Bateman doesn't bother to look up from her puzzle.

                    ANGELA
Hello, mother.

                    LAURIE
Oh, Miss Bateman! I'm Laurie, your mother's caregiver. I am so thrilled to meet you.

                    ANGELA
Hello, Laurie. Mr. Gershwin has told me how helpful you've been.

                    LAURIE
I do the best I can.

Angela then crosses to her mother and stoops to kiss her on the cheek. Mrs. Bateman is as immobile as 'that stone stoop' she alluded to, earlier.

ANGELA

You were asleep when I came in last night, mother. Otherwise, I would have come in to say hello.

MRS. BATEMAN

Nine letter word for one who is not to be trusted. 'C-h-a-r-l-a-t-a-'

ANGELA
(to Laurie)

Why don't you see if Calley will prepare some breakfast for me, Laurie? Would you do that for me, please?

LAURIE

Oh, yes, of course, Miss Bateman. I'll go tell her right this minute.

Laurie hurries back over to the screen door, then turns for a last glimpse of Angela. She sighs, pleasurably, then disappears, inside. Angela walks to the table, lays her script and cell phone down on it then continues on past to the edge of the porch, beyond, looking up at the trees.

ANGELA

I so miss the change of seasons. I forget just how beautiful they are.
(turning back)
How have you been, mother?

MRS. BATEMAN
(still not looking up)

As if you care.

ANGELA

That's not fair, mother. I do care and you know it.

MRS. BATEMAN

That why it's been three years since you've been here for a visit?

Angela then approaches the table looking down at her mother who is still focused on her puzzle.

ANGELA

I come as often as I can. I have a very busy schedule in L.A. You know that.

MRS. BATEMAN

Hmp.

Angela then sits down in one of the chairs.

ANGELA

How long has it been since Marjorie was here? Five years, I believe.

MRS. BATEMAN

None of you come visit me much, anymore. Rawley hasn't been here in ten.

ANGELA

Well, he was living in Europe for most of that time. But, I thought he was here last year?

MRS. BATEMAN
(looking up from the puzzle)

For one night! You call that a visit? And, he spent most of that time out drinkin' with the Bunt boys. I might as well've been dead.

She returns to her puzzle.

ANGELA

Did you get the silk robe and slippers I sent you for your birthday?

MRS. BATEMAN

Yes, I did. Ugliest things I ever saw. I wouldn't be caught dead in 'em.

ANGELA

They were very expensive, mother. I bought them at Niemen's. I don't know why I…

MRS. BATEMAN

You can take 'em back. I don't want 'em.

Angela sighs, then stands and walks back to the porch edge staring out, again.

ANGELA

You have never liked anything I have ever given you, mother.

MRS. BATEMAN

Wrong. I liked those pillows in there you sent me for the divan. And I told you so, too.

ANGELA

You've never liked anything *personal* I've given you.

MRS. BATEMAN

I don't like bein' givin' personal things. Never did.

ANGELA

(turning back)

You liked it when Mercedes *(mer-sah-deez)* gave you personal things.

MRS. BATEMAN
That was different. Mercedes had taste.

ANGELA
Thank you.

MRS. BATEMAN
Just statin' a fact.

ANGELA
Mercedes could never do anything wrong, could she, mother?

MRS. BATEMAN
(looking up, sharply)
Don't you dare use that tone of voice when speaking about that blessed soul.

ANGELA
Mercedes! Mercedes! That's all you've ever thrown in my face, mother. How else am I suppose to speak about her?

MRS. BATEMAN
There never was a more heavenly person on this earth than Mercedes, and that's a fact.
(looking off into the distance)
I can still see her the afternoon they brought her back after she fell off the horse. She was such a *gifted* rider, too. And she was a *wonderful* human being.

ANGELA
(sighing)
I never said she wasn't, mother. It's just that none of your *own* children could ever match up to her in your eyes.

MRS. BATEMAN

After she died that same evenin', somethin' went out of me. I can't explain it but I felt as though a piece of my heart had been ripped right out of my bosom. She was like a cherished sister to me.

ANGELA

And what were Marge and I?

MRS. BATEMAN

What you are now.

ANGELA

And what's that, mother?

MRS. BATEMAN

You tell me. *(pause)* What'd you come all the way here from Hollywood for, anyway?

ANGELA

I came to visit you.

MRS. BATEMAN

You didn't come to visit me. You came to bury me.

Angela ignores the remark. She then walks down to the center of the porch to gather her strength while Mrs. Bateman goes back to the puzzle. After a moment, Angela turns back.

ANGELA

If you must know, mother, I am here for a reason.

MRS. BATEMAN
(looking up, sharply, again)

Ha, the witch speaks.

ANGELA

That was uncalled for and you know it.
(approaching, again)
I love you. I have always loved you. It's just that you have never loved me in return.

MRS. BATEMAN
(back to puzzle)
Four letter word for one who tells *fibs*. 'L-i-a-r!'

ANGELA

Mother...!

MRS. BATEMAN
(bothered, now)
What is it, Angela?

ANGELA

This is very difficult for me. Mr. Gershwin suggested I...

MRS. BATEMAN

Mr. *Gersh*win! I should've guessed as much. He's behind all this, isn't he?

ANGELA

You don't even know what I'm about to say.

MRS. BATEMAN

I don't have to. All I know is you and that shyster lawyer of yours have been plottin' somethin' behind my back for weeks, now, and I am beginnin' to suspect what it might be.

ANGELA

That is not the way to refer to our family lawyer.

MRS. BATEMAN
Who's family lawyer?! Not mine.

ANGELA
Yes, he is *your* lawyer. He is the lawyer who drew up your will and prepared the family trust which you signed, yourself, seven years ago.

MRS. BATEMAN
Which you and he badgered me into. I should never have signed those papers. You call that a livin' will? A livin' hell is what I call it. Besides, I have a lawyer. Mr. Rivenbark is my lawyer. He was my daddy's and he is mine, too.

ANGELA
Mr. Rivenbark did not have the expertise for creating living trusts, mother. Mr. Gershwin is one of the most respected attorneys in this state.

MRS. BATEMAN
And he happens to be in cahoots with you.

Angela goes and sits down, again, at the table.

ANGELA
All that said, there is something we need to discuss. It's time for you to make a change.

MRS. BATEMAN
A change! What kind of change?

ANGELA
You can't go on living here like this.

MRS. BATEMAN
Like what?

ANGELA
You're not all that young anymore and you need help.

MRS. BATEMAN
I *have* help! That's what my caregiver's for.

ANGELA
We've run out of caregivers, mother. Laurie is the last one available. You've driven all the others away.

MRS. BATEMAN
What are you drivin' at, Angela?

ANGELA
We want you to go into a home.

MRS. BATEMAN
A *home*! What kind of a home?

ANGELA
We have found a wonderful facility up in Arkadelphia.

MRS. BATEMAN
I'm not goin' to any old folks home! I was born in this house and I will die in this house. And you and no connivin' shyster lawyer is gonna make me do anything different, ya hear? Old folks home! *Hmp*!

ANGELA
Mother, it is not an old folks home. It is a wonderful assisted-living facility. The food is excellent and there are many women there your age who…

MRS. BATEMAN
You have some nerve, Angela Lynn Bateman. Comin' all the way here from out in California to force me out of my own house and for what purpose I don't know. You could care less whether I live or die.

ANGELA
I am the trustee of your estate. It is my responsibility to see you are taken care of. And I do not have the time to deal with the constant calls I get about your out-of-control behavior.

MRS. BATEMAN
Out-of-control be*hav*ior! What exactly are you referrin' to?!

ANGELA
Let's just say that you have become rather difficult, of late, and I am not that able to deal with, it, anymore. We cannot expect Mr. Gershwin to…

MRS. BATEMAN
Ah-*hah*! It's Gershwin who's put you up to all this, isn't it? I saw him pokin' his nose around here more than once over the past several weeks. Said he was inspectin' the property.

Mrs. Bateman pushes herself away from the table and wheels her chair to the center of the porch.

MRS. BATEMAN (Cont'd)
(staring out)
And just what have you got in *mind* for this house after you've gotten rid of me?

Angela stands and approaches her mother.

ANGELA
The house will be sold.

                    MRS. BATEMAN
Sold!

                    ANGELA
We already have a buyer.

                    MRS. BATEMAN
                    (turning)
Who?!

                    ANGELA
Mr. Gershwin has agreed to purchase the house, himself.

                    MRS. BATEMAN
                    (turning back)
Over my dead *body*! My daddy built this house as a weddin' gift for my mother. No one is gonna sell this house to *anybody*, do you hear me? My daddy promised I could live in this house 'til I die and I'll be damned if I'll go anywhere else before I do! *Ever*! Ya *hear*?

                    ANGELA
Mother, granddaddy did not leave a will. You know that. There was a trust but there was, for some reason, no will. The house was deeded to the trust. There was never any instructions for you to live in the house until you die. The house will be sold and that's final.

Mrs. Bateman stares out in the distance, again, trying to grasp the meaning of all this. The screen door then opens, presently, and Laurie comes back out.

                    LAURIE
Your breakfast is ready, now, Miss Bateman. Would you like to have it out here on the porch?

ANGELA

Well, you need to ask my mother…

MRS. BATEMAN

Never mind me. I'm ready to go back inside, anyway. The air out here has gotten rather foul, of late. I think I'll go take a nap.

LAURIE

Of course, Mrs. Bateman.
(going to the back of her wheelchair)
Shall I tell Calley to bring your breakfast out here, then, Miss Bateman?

ANGELA

Yes, thank you, Laurie. That would be nice.

Laurie proceeds to turn Mrs. Bateman around while Angela opens the screen door for them. Then, Laurie wheels Mrs. Bateman on back inside. Angela closes the screen door, sighs, heavily, and moves past the table to stare out at the trees, again. She is deeply pensive. A moment later, she turns, picking up her cell phone, then punches in a number:

ANGELA
(into phone)
This is Angela Bateman. Is Mark in the office?
(she then sits down in a chair)
Hi, sweetheart! Yes, I got in late last night. So, what day do I start? I haven't had a minute to look at the script. I need a full week in Santa Barbara before… *(pause)* In two *days*?! Are they out of their minds? I can't be ready to start in two days! I need more time than that. Don't they know I always have written in my contracts… *(pause)* I know this is not a studio picture, but… *(pause)* Well, the reason I haven't worked in two years is because
(Cont'd)

                    ANGELA (Cont's)
the scripts I've been given aren't what they... *(pause)* I know it's
not easy finding rolls for actresses my age. You don't have to
bring that up... *(pause)* Of course, I want to do this picture. I just
need more time... *(pause, sighing)* All right. I'll be ready to start
in two days. *(again, a pause)* No, no. I'm... okay. Everything's
fine. I'll be leaving here, tonight. I'm dropping mother off, on my
way, then I'm heading for the airport, after that. We can touch
base, again, in the morning... *(pause)* Of course, I appreciate what
you're doing for me. You know that. You're the best agent in
town. I've always said so. It's just... well, it's just... things aren't
as easy as they used to be, that's all. *(pause)* I do appreciate you,
Mark. More than you know. *(pause)* Yes, I'll call when I get
back. Thank you.

She punches off then places the phone down, anguish on her face. Then, she picks up the script. She is just about to thumb through it when the screen door flies open from a kick. Charlene comes out carrying a tray with Angela's breakfast on it.

                    CHARLENE
Hi, hun!

                    ANGELA
                (looking around)
Oh, Charlene! I didn't even know you were over here.

Charlene approaches the table placing the tray down before Angela.

                    CHARLENE
I came over to bring your mother some of Franklin's sweet
potatoes. I thought Calley could cook up a mess of 'em for supper,
tonight. Calley's got her hands full, right now, so I said I'd bring
your breakfast with me on my way out the door.

ANGELA

Thanks, Charlene. You're an angel.

CHARLENE

Now, give me a hug.

Angela half stands and the two hug and kiss on the cheeks. Angela then sits back down and Charlene follows, sitting in a chair, opposite. Angela proceeds to pour herself a cup of tea from the tea pot, then takes a sip from her cup.

CHARLENE (Cont'd)

How was your flight, hun?

ANGELA

I had to change planes in Saint Louis *(louie),* as usual. But, other than that, no problem.

CHARLENE

Well, that's right precious. We didn't even know you were comin.' I haven't even had a chance to call all the girls.

ANGELA

Well, don't. I'm flying back out, this evening.

CHARLENE

This *evenin'*?! My heavenly days! We won't even have time for a proper visit.

ANGELA

Well, I couldn't afford to even make the trip, time-wise. But, Mr. Gershwin—you know, our lawyer—he absolutely insisted. It's about mother.

CHARLENE

I heard.

ANGELA
(sighing)
I have no other choice.

CHARLENE
What do you mean?

ANGELA
Well, she's getting rather out-of-control.

CHARLENE
Really…?

ANGELA
She fires the caregivers just as quick as Mr. Gershwin can find them. And, to tell you the truth, Charlene, there just aren't any more available, around here. This one, Laurie's her name…

CHARLENE
Yes, we've met. This morning, actually.

ANGELA
Well, she's our last possibility. So, Mr. Gershwin recommended mother go into an assisted living facility up in Arkadelphia, instead.

CHARLENE
I heard that, too. But, Angela, I don't think your mother's ready for that. I mean she seems to be doin' all right livin' here.

ANGELA
It's not that simple, Charlene. The problem isn't living here in this house. And the problem is keeping someone here with her. Oh, you don't know the whole of it. It's been a nightmare. Your mother's lucky to have you and Franklin able to live in with her. My mother… well, that's a different story, altogether.

CHARLENE
I know Mrs. Bateman can be difficult at times, but…

ANGELA
I just don't have the patience for it, anymore. I'm starting a new picture in two days and all I get are calls from the lawyer about mother doing this or that, or not doing something she was supposed to do. And I have no help at all, you know.

CHARLENE
You mean, from Marge?

ANGELA
Well, who else? It's all on my shoulders, you know. Of course, I'm the trustee of the estate. But, Marge has washed her hands of everything and it's all my responsibility. I just don't have the time for it, anymore.

CHARLENE
Are you two still not talkin'?

ANGELA
You mean Marge and I? I prefer it that way.

CHARLENE
And what does your brother think about all this?

ANGELA
Rawley has stayed out of it and always has. I don't blame him, but I can't depend on him for anything, either.

CHARLENE
(sighing)
Well. I just wish there were another way.

ANGELA

I'm afraid there isn't.

Angela then sips more of her tea. After a moment,

CHARLENE

Angela, I thought your mother's lawyer was Mr. Rivenbark over on Chestnut Street.

ANGELA

He used to be.

CHARLENE

Wasn't he Judge Bateman's lawyer, too?

ANGELA

Yes. But, when we created the trust, we needed a lawyer who specialized in that sort of thing and that's when I hired Mr. Gershwin. He's very respected.

CHARLENE

I know that. But, do you think he has your mother's best interests in mind?

ANGELA

What do you mean by that, Charlene? Of course, he does.

CHARLENE

Well, I mean it's just that Mr. Rivenbark was always a friend of the family, and all.

ANGELA

There are no friends when it comes to lawyers, Charlene. Believe me, Hollywood has taught me that if nothing else.

CHARLENE
Well, what if your mother refuses to go?

ANGELA
Then, I'll have to have her declared incompetent.

CHARLENE
Incompetent! That might be a little difficult to do. You know, your mother's sharp as a tack, Angela. She's won every crossword puzzle contest the paper's ever held.

ANGELA
Don't worry. I'm sure Mr. Gershwin can take care of it. *(pause)* How's Franklin?

CHARLENE
Fine.

ANGELA
And, your mother?

CHARLENE
Oh, just fine.

ANGELA
Tell them, both, I said hello.

CHARLENE
I surely will. I wish you were stayin' a little longer, though. Everything's happenin' so fast around here.

ANGELA
Well, it's been in the works for weeks. Let's just say, today it's final.

Charlene stiffens as the truth sinks in.

CHARLENE
I understand. *(sighing)* What's your new movie about?

ANGELA
(amused at herself)
It's called 'Mrs. Forrester's Weekend.' A woman in jeopardy. I'm tied up for most of the movie.

CHARLENE
Oh, my Lord! That doesn't sound like fun.

ANGELA
Why not? The male lead's a total unknown and oh is he *gorgeous*.

CHARLENE
Is he the one who ties you up?

ANGELA
Who else?

CHARLENE
Well, that's right precious.
(standing up)
Now, I've just got to get goin'.

ANGELA
(Angela stands, as well)
If I don't see you before I leave, you take care of yourself, all right?

CHARLENE
I'm sure I'll be back over before you go.

The screen door opens and Laurie comes back out.

LAURIE
(to Charlene)
Oh, *you* brought Miss Bateman's breakfast out…

CHARLENE
I was on my way out, anyway. *(leaving)* See y'all later.

Charlene hurries down the steps and walk, disappearing offstage. Angela then picks up her cell phone and her mother's empty coffee mug, placing them both on the tray. Then, she picks the tray up.

ANGELA
I thought I was hungry but I guess I'm not.

LAURIE
Oh, I'll take all that in for you, Miss Bateman.

ANGELA
Nonsense. I can take it in, myself. Just get the screen door for me, Laurie, will you?

LAURIE
Oh, yes, of course, Miss Bateman.

Laurie hurries to open the screen door and, as Angela goes back inside with the tray, Laurie watches her every move with awe. Then, she closes the screen door, sighing pleasurably, once more. After that, she turns and moves across to the table where she spies the script laying there. Out of burning curiosity, the picks it up.

LAURIE
(reading title out loud)
'Mrs. Forrester's Weekend.'

Then, she opens the script and is, immediately, drawn to a bit of dialogue.

LAURIE (Cont'd)
(again, out loud)
'Are you just gonna leave me like this, young man? Or are you gonna keep me tied up the whole weekend long? *(sighing pleasurably, again, then pretending to be acting)* 'I *am* a *woman*, you know?'

Laurie then, dreamily, sinks into a chair clutching the script to her bosom as the lights fade out.

Scene Two

Same scene as before. At curtain's rise, no one is on the porch or in the yard as a gentle breeze is rustling the leaves. The time is mid-day. Then, we hear voices, offstage, from up the front walk:

MARGE (OS)
I don't know what I would've done if your plane hadn't gotten in 'bout the same time as mine, Rawley. I just don't have money to be renting a car, even for a couple of days.

MARGEORIE BATEMAN GENNY, a plump, yet pretty woman, a couple of years younger than her sister Angela, with short, bleached blonde hair and wearing a winter outfit with heels, is carrying a small suitcase as she is coming up to the house. She is followed by her brother RAWLEY BATEMAN who is much younger than either of his two sisters by, at least, five years. He is mildly attractive and polite in the Southern tradition. He wears casual clothes with jacket and is, likewise, carrying a small suitcase, in hand.

MARGE (Cont'd)
You must've known I'd be coming in at that time.

RAWLEY

No, Marge. I didn't know that, at all. I was just as surprised as you.

MARGE

Well, I appreciate bein' able to ride down here with you. You're my dear, dear little brother.

RAWLEY

I was glad I could give you a lift.

MARGE

Well...

As the two reach the front steps, Marge stops.

MARGE (Cont'd)

How long have you known about mother?

RAWLEY
(stopping, as well)

About her recent fall?

MARGE

No... this idea of Angela's to put her in some rest home, somewhere. Did you know about that, before recently?

RAWLEY

I didn't know anything until Angela called and asked me to come home.

MARGE

Well, I didn't know anything about it, either. But, what else is new? Angela never tells me, anything 'bout anything. You know that.

                    RAWLEY
That's only because you two are not talking to each other, anymore.

                    MARGE
Does she ever tell you anything?

                    RAWLEY
No. But, then, it's usually not my responsibility.

                    MARGE
Rawley! How could you say a thing like that? It's both our responsibilities and you know that. We are talkin' about our dear mother.

                    RAWLEY
That's not what I meant, Marge. Angela's the trustee of the estate, not me... and not you either. It's her responsibility and not...

                    MARGE
I know she's in control of everything. But, I have told her a thousand times or more I would gladly come here and take care of mother if she would just...

                    RAWLEY
                (starts up the steps)
Mother doesn't *want* you here, Marge.

                    MARGE
                (following up)
I *know* what elderly people need, Rawley. And, my mother needs me. I know she does.

                    RAWLEY
            (stopping midway, sighing, heavily)
I don't wanna talk about it. I'm tired and I just wanna...

The screen door opens and Laurie comes out onto the porch.

> MARGE
> *(looking up at her)*
> Well, who in the world are *you*?!

> LAURIE
> *(feeling confronted)*
> I'm… I'm Mrs. Bateman's caregiver. Can I help you…?

Marge continues up the steps with Rawley following after her.

> MARGE
> What happened to Sarah Jane? I thought…

> LAURIE
> She was Mrs. Bateman's caregiver, before me. Can I help you with something?

> MARGE
> Well, I hope *so*! I'm Marge, Mrs. Bateman's daughter. And this is my brother Rawley.

> LAURIE
> *Oh*! I'm *so sorry*. I didn't know y'all were comin'. You want me to take your bag?

> MARGE
> Thank you. That would be helpful.

The two siblings have reached the porch and Marge hands her bag to Laurie.

> MARGE ((Cont'd)
> Where's my mother?

LAURIE
She's in her room takin' a nap. I know she's gonna be just thrilled t'death when she finds out you two are here.

MARGE
Has Angela gotten here yet?

LAURIE
Yes, ma'am. She came in late last night. I got to meet her this mornin'. I was just in a tether. I've never met a real movie star, before.

MARGE
Well, I'd like to talk to her before I see my mother.

RAWLEY
Marge… now don't go starting anything…

MARGE
I know what I'm doin', Rawley. My mother needs me and I need to find out just what Angela's got in mind, here.

RAWLEY
Can't that wait until we get settled in?

MARGE
I wanna take care of it, now, and prevent anything drastic happenin' before it's too late.
(to Laurie)
What do *you* know about any of this?

LAURIE
Well, not very much, if you mean what I know about your mother.

MARGE
Did Angela say when she plans to have my mother taken away?

LAURIE
Well, I understand… I mean…

MARGE
(glancing at Rawley)
This is why we need to get on this, right away.

RAWLEY
I'm not gettin' involved, here.

MARGE
Then, why in the world did you come home?

RAWLEY
Because Angela asked me to come, that's why. I told you that, before.

MARGE
My mother is needin' me to come to her defense, Rawley, and we both have to take a stand, here.

RAWLEY
Marge, you don't even know what's goin' on. You should wait 'til Angela has a chance to tell us more about what's happenin', first.

MARGE
That is *exactly* what I am tryin' to do.
(to Laurie)
Will you go tell Angela that Marge and Rawley are out here on the porch and we want her to come out and talk to us, please?

LAURIE
Yes, Miss Bateman.

MARGE
Genny.

LAURIE
I'm sorry...?

MARGE
My married name is Genny. I was married... before. My name is... Genny.

LAURIE
Oh, I'm sorry, Miss... Genny. I'll go and tell Miss Bateman you wanna see her, right away.

Laurie then disappears into the house, again, with Marge's suitcase. Rawley then crosses to the table, sits his bag down and takes a seat in one of the chairs. Marge then goes back to the steps, gazing out at the yard.

MARGE
This place is a wreck. Abraham must be getting' too old to keep the yard up, any longer.

RAWLEY
It's fall, Marge. It's supposed to look like that.

MARGE
Well, it looks just awful, to me. I can remember there was shrubbery all around here.

RAWLEY
Those shrubs have not been here for eons. Mother had them all taken out. I know they weren't here when I came home the last time.

MARGE
Well, I don't know why she'd go and have that done. It just makes the place look bare. Looks like a boarding house, to me.

RAWLEY

Fine. Have it your way.

MARGE
(turning and approaching him)
I guess you're for all this, then.

RAWLEY

I didn't say that. It's just that...

MARGE

You know very well I could come live here with mother and she wouldn't need...

RAWLEY

Marge, don't start that, again. We've been through that a hundred times, over. Mother does not want you livin' here with her and you know that.

MARGE

I *know*. I *know*.

Marge then walks past the table to look out at the same trees Angela did, earlier.

MARGE (Con't)

My whole life I've had to accept that. It hasn't been easy for me I won't you to know. I love my mother, dearly.

Silence ensues except for the rustle of the trees. Then, a voice is heard within.

ANGELA (OS.)

Please tell Calley that my sister and brother are here, will you, Laurie? She'll need to prepare them some lunch.

LAURIE (OS.)
I will do that, Miss Bateman.

Marge turns as Angela is coming out the screen door.

ANGELA
Hello to you both. And I want to thank you for coming home at this sensitive time.

RAWLEY
(standing up)
Glad we could be here.

MARGE
Well, I, for one, wanna know just exactly what's goin' on.

ANGELA
Didn't Rawley tell you anything?

MARGE
(approaching her)
All I know is you're puttin' mother in a rest home and you haven't consulted anybody else about it.

ANGELA
That's precisely why I asked you to come home, Marge.

MARGE
So, you're *not* puttin' her in a home, then?

ANGELA
I didn't say that. She *has* to go into a retirement facility. I just thought you'd like to be here when it happens.

MARGE

Well, I think you should have discussed it with me, first. She's *my* mother and...

RAWLEY

Marge!

MARGE
(turning to him)

What...?

RAWLEY

She's *our* mother, too. You keep talkin' as if...

MARGE

I know she's *your* mother, too! But, I seem to be the only one here who's showing any concern for her.

ANGELA

I don't have time for this, Marge. I have to fly back to L.A., this evening, and I don't want to deal with your...

MARGE

With my what?! My interference?

ANGELA

I have a responsibility to see that mother is taken care of. She already fell and broke one of her hips, three years ago. Now, she's fallen, again, and thank God it's only a mild fracture, this time. But, she can't go on like...

MARGE

That's exactly what I wanna talk to you about.

Marge crosses past Angela, then turns back

MARGE (Cont'd)
I agree mother cannot live by herself, anymore. That's why it's time for me to move back home and start takin' care of her, myself.

ANGELA
She doesn't want you taking care of her, Marge! She can't stand you being here more than one day at a time!

MARGE
That's because you have undermined me with her ever since I can remember!

RAWLEY
Marge, mother has told you, herself, over and over, again, she does not want you living here with her. Why can't you accept that?

MARGE
(turning his way)
She would get used to it.

ANGELA
No one would get used to that!

MARGE
(turning back)
You think you are so above everything, Angela. My dear mother needs me and I am determined to prove to you that you are wrong about it.

Now, Angela walks past the table to the porch edge, staring out at the trees, again.

ANGELA
Everything has been arranged. I don't want to discuss it, any further.

MARGE

What do you mean by that?

Rawley picks up his bag then crosses to the screen door.

ANGELA
(directly to Marge)
I mean that Mr. Gershwin has arranged for mother to go into The Good Shepherd Retirement Home up in Arkadelphia, that's what.

MARGE

When?!

ANGELA

I'm taking her there, myself... this afternoon.

Rawley and Marge exchange a look, then he heads on into the house.

MARGE

I *don't* think that's fair, Angela?

ANGELA

Fair?

MARGE

Yes, fair! Don't you think I should have some say in this?

ANGELA

Marge, you have been out of any of this for years. I am the only one who has to deal with it and...

MARGE

That's because you took over and made yourself in control of everything.

ANGELA

If you're talking about the trust, mother agreed to all that and she wanted me to act as her trustee.

MARGE

That's not what I understood happened.

ANGELA

What do you mean?

MARGE

I understood *you* suggested you act as trustee and...

ANGELA

Well, I don't care what you understood, Marge...

MARGE

No, you never have! It's always been Angela! Angela got her way with everything! You got to go to college, not me. It was always you, Angela. Always! I never got anything except your hand-me-downs!

ANGELA

If I remember right, you dropped out of college after one semester.

MARGE

That was hardly a college, Angela.

ANGELA

State Teacher's College is a very respected school!

MARGE

Now, it is! Back then, it was a two-year backwater where you ended up if you didn't have the money to go anywhere else. I hated every minute of it. But, *you*! *You* got to go to the uni*versity*!

ANGELA
You didn't have the grades to get into the university, Marge, and you know it.

MARGE
I could've gotten in somewhere else!

Angela goes to the table and sits down in one of the chairs.

ANGELA
That is not why we are here.

MARGE
That is *exactly* why we are here. The big *star* has come home to shut her mother away in some pathetic old folks home and we get no say so in any of it, as *usual*!

Angela buries her head in her hands out of exhaustion. After sighing, heavily, she gets up and heads for the screen door.

ANGELA
I need to lie down for a while. *(calling)* Laurie!

LAURIE (OS)
(calling back)
Yes, Miss Bateman?

Laurie then comes out the screen door.

ANGELA
I'm going to lie down upstairs for a while. If anyone calls from Hollywood, I want to know about it, right away. Otherwise, I'd rather not be disturbed.

LAURIE
Yes, Miss Bateman. Can I get you anything?

ANGELA
No, thank you. I just need some time by myself.

Laurie then holds the screen door open as Angela disappears inside, then she follows in, afterwards. Marge stares after the two, then crosses to the screen door, as well, jerks it open and enters, slamming it behind her. The lights then fade out.

Scene Three

Same scene as before. At curtain's rise, Mrs. Bateman is, once again, in her wheelchair which is now parked out in the yard. She is wearing the shawl over her shoulders, again, and is, likewise, wielding her trusted cane. Abraham stands, nearby, holding a gardener's spade, in hand. The time is afternoon.

MRS. BATEMAN
Abraham, what do you see there at the edge of my porch?

ABRAHAM
(looking hard, then scratching his head)
Well, Miss Bettye, I don't know just what y'all means?

MRS. BATEMAN
Look again. You see my jonquils, there? My *jonquils*, Abraham! What's left of 'em.

ABRAHAM
Why, sho'nuf, Mrs. Bettye. I sees 'em.

MRS. BATEMAN
Well, Abraham, we've got to do somethin' 'bout them, this minute.

ABRAHAM
Now, Miss Belttye, whats ya'll means we gots t'do?

MRS. BATEMAN
I mean we've got to do somethin' to protect them, that's what I mean. Don't you remember last Halloween? One of those little devils went and trampled all over my jonquils and they liked to never've come up in the spring? If I'd caught that little rascal red handed, why I would've yanked every hair out of his tiny little head.

ABRAHAM
Oh, now, Miss Bettye! Would ya'll've done such a thing?

MRS. BATEMAN
In a hair-splittin' second I would have! I am very attached to my jonquils, Abraham, and you know that.

ABRAHAM
Oh, I knows that. I sho do knows that. Ya'll is real attached to them jonquils.

MRS. BATEMAN
Well, we have to protect 'em. I want no tricks played on me, this year. No nasty tricks with my jonquils, ya hear?

ABRAHAM
Yes, Miss Bettye. I hears y'all. But, what is we all gonna do?

MRS. BATEMAN
I'll tell you what we're gonna do. I want you to go bring back some of those leaves you've been rakin' up, 'round here.

ABRAHAM
Bring 'em back! Now, Miss Bettye, why would you want me to do that? I just spent the whole mornin' rakin' up those leaves, and…

MRS. BATEMAN
'Cause I want you to use 'em to cover up my jonquils, that's why. That way, if they get trampled on, this year, it won't matter all that much, I presume.

ABRAHAM
I sees, now. That might just be a good idea, after all. I will do that. I sho will do that.

MRS. BATEMAN
(pointing with her cane)
And I want you to do the same with my petunias 'round there on the side of the porch, ya hear?

ABRAHAM
Yes, Miss Bettye. I will do that, too.

MRS. BATEMAN
I don't want to see my petunias trampled on, either.

ABRAHAM
No, Miss Bettye. We got t'protect them petunias, too.

MRS. BATEMAN
(then, looking around the yard)
Now, I think that oughta just about do it.

ABRAHAM
Yes, Miss Bettye. That oughta just about do it, sho'nuf.

MRS. BATEMAN
Would you then be so kind as to wheel me back up onto the porch? I don't know where in hell that Laurie's gone to? She is never 'round here when I need her.

ABRAHAM
Yes, Miss Bettye. I'll get ya'll right back up on the po'ch, this very minute.

Abraham sticks the spade into his back pocket then goes to the back of the wheelchair and begins pushing Mrs. Bateman gently up the ramp.

MRS. BATEMAN
(going up)
Abraham, have you heard what my daughter's got in mind for her mother?

ABRAHAM
Well, Miss Bettye, I haves. Yes, I haves.

MRS. BATEMAN
And what do you think about it, Abraham?

ABRAHAM
Well, Miss Bettye, I thinks it's a shame.

MRS. BATEMAN
You do?

ABRAHAM
Yes, ma'am, I sho do. I thinks it's a real shame.

They reach the porch where Abraham then wheels the chair to the center, leaving it parked, there.

MRS. BATEMAN
You know, my daddy always said I could live here in this house 'til I die?

ABRAHAM
Oh, yes, Miss Bettye, he sho did. I done heard Judge Bateman say that *a hun'ed* times. He sho'nuf did.

MRS. BATEMAN
But, my daughter's got it in her head to put me in some old folks home, instead.

ABRAHAM
I knows that, Miss Bettye. What is ya'lls gonna do?

MRS. BATEMAN
I don't know, Abraham. But, I wish I did.

ABRAHAM
Oh, Miss Bettye, I feels awful bad.

MRS. BATEMAN
I know, Abraham. I know just how you feel. You're in as big o'mess as I am, aren't you? We are two peas in a pod and somebody's gettin' good and ready to cook us both.

ABRAHAM
They sho is, Miss Bettye. They sho is.

Laurie then comes out the screen door holding a glass of bourbon in hand.

LAURIE
Calley thought you might like your bourbon out here, Mrs. Bateman. I told her it was gettin' kinda cold, but she said you like you're bourbon out here on the porch every afternoon, whether it's swelterin' hot or freezin' cold. Is that true?

MRS. BATEMAN
It is true, Laurie. Be so kind as to put it over there on the table for me, please.

Laurie then heads for the table sitting the glass down while Abraham pushes Mrs. Bateman to the table, as well. Mrs. Bateman then picks up the glass and drinks nearly a fourth of it before sitting it down, again.

MRS. BATEMAN (Cont'd)
Now, *that* is a delight. Nothin' better than a nice, smooth glass of bourbon to settle your nerves... right, Abraham?

ABRAHAM
Oh, yes, Miss Bettye. That is right. That is sho'nuf right.

MRS. BATEMAN
Have you seen my daughter this afternoon, Laurie?

LAURIE
No, I haven't, Mrs. Bateman. I think she's lyin' down, upstairs. At least, that's what she told me she was gonna do. 'Course that was a good hour or so ago and it's goin' on two o'clock, I believe.

MRS. BATEMAN
You better go on and get to my jonquils, Abraham 'fore it gets too late.

ABRAHAM
Yes, ma'am. I am goin'. I am goin', right this minute.

MRS. BATEMAN
We've got to protect my jonquils.

ABRAHAM
And yo petunias, too.

MRS. BATEMAN
And my petunias, too, Abraham.

ABRAHAM

I am goin', right now.

Abraham then hurries, stepping off the end of the porch and disappearing to the back.

MRS. BATEMAN

Have you noticed, Laurie, where this porch faces?

LAURIE

You mean toward the south, Mrs. Bateman?

MRS. BATEMAN

I do. My daddy always said a porch with a southern exposure is like havin' summer the whole year long. And he was right. And that is why I come out here every afternoon and that's why I take my bourbon out here, too, no matter how cold it gets.

LAURIE

I *see*. Why, I'm beginnin' to feel warmer, already.

Mrs. Bateman drinks more of her bourbon before sitting the glass down, again. Then, she looks up at the trees, reflecting a moment.

MRS. BATEMAN

You know something,' Laurie, over these many years this old house has become a part of me. Or, maybe I've become a part of it, I'm not rightly sure. But, I can tell you one thing, I just cannot envision my ever livin' anywhere else.

LAURIE

Oh, Mrs. Bateman, I know just how you feel.

MRS. BATEMAN
I don't see how you could. I don't think anyone knows what it is like unless a house has been a part of them since the day they were born into it. For me, this house has taken on a character of its own.
(looking back at Laurie)
Did you know I sometimes talk to it?

LAURIE
To this *house*?

MRS. BATEMAN
Yes, I do. This house knows every one of my secrets, Laurie, and I know all of its secrets, too. We are bonded together like two life-long lovers who's souls have grown into one.

LAURIE
What kind of things do you say to this house, Mrs. Bateman?

MRS. BATEMAN
Oh, most times I tell it just how much it has meant to me. But, sometimes, I tell it about a problem I might be trying to solve at the time and I ask it if it has any ideas about solvin' it.

LAURIE
And does it answer you?

MRS. BATEMAN
Well, not in words, of course. But, often, after a short time, I feel a great comfort comin' on and, in no time, the solution just comes starin' me right in the face. And I say to it, "Old house, you have come through for me, again, and I thank you for it."

LAURIE
That's just wonderful, Mrs. Bateman.

MRS. BATEMAN

You know, when I was 'bout nine years old, my daddy—that was Judge Bateman—he had me built a playhouse *(pointing with cane)* right out there in the side yard under those big old pecan trees. And, would you believe it, it looked just like this old house only in miniature?

LAURIE

Oh, how adorable!

MRS. BATEMAN

It had a little porch just like this big one. And, all the windows had real glass panes and went up and down just like the ones, here. And the floors were real hardwood, too.

LAURIE

Oh, my word!

MRS. BATEMAN

That wasn't the half of it. It had a little staircase with a curved banister that led upstairs to a tiny little room where I kept all my dolls. And my best friend Julia Mae Guthrie—that's Charlene's mother, next door—she would come over every afternoon and we would play house from noon 'til suppertime.

LAURIE

That must have been a wonderful time for you, Mrs. Bateman.

MRS. BATEMAN

Oh, it was. *(sighing)* It certainly was.

LAURIE

What happened to it, Mrs. Bateman? I mean to your little playhouse? Where is it, now?

MRS. BATEMAN

Gone.

LAURIE

Torn down?

MRS. BATEMAN

No. We had a terrible rainstorm, one year. Thunder and lightnin' like you have never seen. We all thought the house was gonna fall down, it shook so bad. Mother was more frightened than I. She always hated storms, you see. I remember I was peekin' out the upstairs window, even though I had been told to stay well away from windows durin' electrical storms. But, there I was, peekin' out at my playhouse when all of a sudden this lightin' bolt came right down out of the sky, struck one of those pecan trees splittin' it down the middle and proceeded right on across to my playhouse, striking it, too. Both the tree and the playhouse burst into flames. I just stood there starin' in disbelief, watchin' my playhouse burn down until it was completely gone.

LAURIE

Oh, Mrs. Bateman! I'm *so* sorry. That must have been a terrible trauma for you.

MRS. BATEMAN

No, not really. I was 'bout twelve, then, and done playin' house, you see. But, I was thankful the Lord had chosen to take my playhouse instead of this one. I never gave it another thought. I loved my playhouse but it was never a part of me like this old house has been. And, that is why I just can't imagine livin' anywhere else.

LAURIE

Isn't there somethin' somebody can do, Mrs. Bateman? I mean 'bout seein' that you can stay here in your house for as long as you want?

MRS. BATEMAN
(looking directly at her)
Tell me somethin', Laurie? Have you ever wanted to have children?

LAURIE
Oh, *yes*, Mrs. Bateman. I would *love* to have children of my own, one day. I have always wanted to have children.

MRS. BATEMAN
Well, it is not all it's made out to be. Take my word for it. Children grow up and they have lives of their own, and when you get in their way… well, you just become expendable.

LAURIE
Oh, Mrs. Bateman. I am *so, so* sorry.

MRS. BATEMAN
I'm through with my bourbon, Laurie. Would you take the glass back inside for me? And, would you be so kind as to tell my daughter Angela I'd like to see her out here on the porch.

LAURIE
Yes, Mrs. Bateman. I will.

Laurie picks up the bourbon glass and goes back inside through the screen door. Mrs. Bateman then stares out, pondering. Abraham comes back around to the front carrying the apple basket full of raked leaves.

ABRAHAM
I gots the leaves fo'ya'll's jonquils, Miss Bettye. I am gonna cover 'em up for ya'll, real good. Real good.

Abraham then proceeds to pour the leaves along the edge of the porch while humming. After he has finished with the jonquils, Mrs

Bateman looks over.

MRS. BATEMAN
That's just as I want it, Abraham. Thank you. Thank you for all you've ever done for me.

ABRAHAM
Oh, now, Miss Bettye, don't need t'go thankin' me fo'nothin.' It is my thing to do.

MRS. BATEMAN
And, you have done it so very well, Abraham.

ABRAHAM
Yes, Miss Bettye. I trys. Sho'nuf, I trys.

Abraham then continues on around to the side where he pours the rest of the leaves over the petunias. Then, he disappears on to the back. The screen door opens, presently, and Angela comes out. She is carrying her script in hand, open to a page as if she has been reading it, inside.

ANGELA
You wanted to see me, mother?

Angela then walks to the table, laying the script down on it then continuing on to the porch edge, looking out. Mrs. Bateman stares down at the script.

MRS. BATEMAN
You know, you could have had a brilliant career, Angela?

Angela turns back.

MRS. BATEMAN (Cont'd)
You could have worked for the State Department in Washington like Evelyn Horton's mother did… gone all over the world, too. After all, you majored in government, I remember.

ANGELA
I have a career, mother. And I've done quite well with it.

MRS. BATEMAN
Actin' is not a career, Angela. Not a respected one, anyway.

ANGELA
Mother, please.

MRS. BATEMAN
None of you have ever pursued your full potential. Marjorie, up there in Connecticut makin' those ridiculous clay pots. Disgraceful. And, Rawley… well, who knows what he does? Bartendin' in one of those *special* kind of bars.

ANGELA
He is a writer, mother.

MRS. BATEMAN
Writer! Just when did he ever make a dime at that?

ANGELA
It is his calling. We all follow what we feel we need to pursue.

MRS. BATEMAN
No, you just avoid what you really ought to be pursuin'; goin' off chasin' after some childish dreams. You out in Hollywood. Marjorie livin' the life of a bohemian and Rawley just wastin' his life, first in New Orleans *(nu-awlins)*, then Paris and now up in New York. Not a one of you have ever achieved your potential and you know it.

ANGELA

No, I don't know it, mother. I think I've done quite well with my... career.

MRS. BATEMAN

You would.

Angela walks down to the center of the porch staring outward, from there.

ANGELA

You've always been hard on all of us, mother. Especially daddy.

MRS. BATEMAN

Don't bring him into this. He's dead, anyway.

ANGELA
(turning back)

Why not? I think he deserves mention, here. You never gave him a chance, either.

MRS. BATEMAN

He never had it in him.

ANGELA

That's not true. He had a lot in him. You just refused to ever recognize it.

MRS. BATEMAN

And just what do you mean by that?

ANGELA
(approaching her)

For one thing, he was an excellent archer.

MRS. BATEMAN

He was a good one.

ANGELA

No, mother, he was excellent! He was state champion, he was tri-state champion and he was fourth in the nationals. He was *excellent*!

MRS. BATEMAN

I never denied it.

ANGELA

No. You just ignored it, that's all. And when he collected one too many trophies for it— all lined up on the piano, in there—you decided to go and have them thrown out when he was away. What did you do that for, mother?

MRS. BATEMAN

Did you ever try dustin' those things?

ANGELA

No, I did not and neither did you. You've never had a dust cloth in your hand in your whole life. You threw them out because you were jealous, that's why.

MRS. BATEMAN

That's absurd.

ANGELA

Is it?

MRS. BATEMAN

Of course it is. I had a few trophies of my own, if you recall. I was a pretty good archer, myself, in those days. Mine got thrown out along with his.

ANGELA

But, yours didn't mean to you what his meant to him. That's the difference. *(sitting down at the table, opposite her)* That broke him and you know it. Why did you do that, mother? *Why?*

MRS. BATEMAN

Don't torture me, Angela! I don't know why I did it.

ANGELA

I'll tell you why. Because he didn't make a living at it. That's why. No one could ever please you, mother, with that. No one could ever please you because no one could ever live up to your expectations with it. Neither Marge nor I could ever be the daughters you wanted. We were never smart enough, pretty enough, gracious enough. We were never *Mercedes.*

Angela then buries her head in her hands. After a moment, Mrs. Bateman turns and wheels her chair to the porch center, looking out, again.

MRS. BATEMAN

Why have you come here?

ANGELA

(looking up)

I told you, I'm here because…

MRS. BATEMAN

Yes, yes, I know all that. But, why are we havin' this conversation? Can't you just do your dirty work and be done with it? Must you punish me while you're at it?

ANGELA

I thought we might, at least, try to become friends.

MRS. BATEMAN
Friends! (turning and staring back) ...Oh, you picked a fine time for *that*.

Mrs. Bateman then wheels herself back toward Angela.

MRS. BATEMAN (Cont'd)
Did I ever tell you why I never went to college?

ANGELA
(perplexed)
No. I just thought you never wanted to.

MRS. BATEMAN
Oh, how wrong you were, Angela. How very wrong you were.

ANGELA
You mean you wanted to go?

MRS. BATEMAN
Of *course* I wanted to go. How could you think anything different? I *lived* for it!

ANGELA
Well, I...

MRS. BATEMAN
In my senior year of high school, we had visitors—representatives from various colleges and universities—who came through. That's the way they did it, back then. And, all of my girlfriends had plans to go off to colleges throughout the South. University of Alabama, Mississippi. Arkansas. Some were even plannin' on goin' down to Tulane. But, that wasn't good enough for me. No. *I* wanted to go to *Vassar*.

ANGELA

Vassar!

MRS. BATEMAN

Yes, Vassar. So, I asked my daddy if he would send me to Vassar and he told me of course he would. I went back to school and told all my girlfriends my daddy was sendin' me to *Vassar*. I was so proud of that. And, Mrs. Peabody, our principle, took me aside and asked me, "Bettye Lynn, are you sure about that? Are you sure your daddy's gonna send you to Vassar?" And I told her yes, I was. "My daddy told me so." And when it came time to put in our applications, I went back to him and, do you know what he said to me?

Angela stares, in silence.

MRS. BATEMAN (Cont'd)

"*Vassar!*" he said. Then, he started laughin.' He laughed and laughed so hard I thought he was gonna have a stroke. "Why in the world would I send you to *Vassar*?" he asked. 'I've got two sons I've got to send off to college. Why in the world would I send *you* to *Vassar*?"

ANGELA

Oh, mother…

MRS. BATEMAN

I never went back to school, after that.

ANGELA

You mean you didn't graduate?

Now, Mrs. Bateman is silent. It is clear the answer is no.

ANGELA (Cont'd)

I had no idea.

MRS. BATEMAN
I thought, at least, one of you would do somethin' meanin'ful with your life... even if I hadn't. I prayed for that.

Angela then stands and walks back to the edge of the porch looking out, again. After a moment,

ANGELA
I know what that must have done to you, mother. And I'm so very sorry.

MRS. BATEMAN
Well, it's just one of those things that happens, that's all.

ANGELA
(turning back)
Don't you see, though, how that has crippled you? We all wanted so much to love you. And, most of all, we wanted you to love us, in return. But, when none of us could ever live up to your expectations, you punished us. You rejected us because of it.
(approaching)
It didn't have to be that way. I wish I had only known.

After a long silence,

ANGELA (Cont'd)
I'll have Laurie pack your bag
.

MRS. BATEMAN
(taken aback)
What...?

ANGELA
Mr. Gershwin is sending a limo at four o'clock, this afternoon. I'm taking you to Arkadelphia, myself. Then, I'll be going on to the airport, from there.

MRS. BATEMAN
(stunned)
I see.

ANGELA
The facility is sending someone down, next week, to pick up the rest of your things.

MRS. BATEMAN
The rest of my things...

ANGELA
Well, yes. The things you'll need once you're there.

MRS. BATEMAN
And you think they'll know what that will be...?

ANGELA
Well, yes, of course. They'll know.

MRS. BATEMAN
I see...

Angela picks up her script then walks toward the screen door.

ANGELA
There isn't much time. I need to start packing, myself.

Angela then opens it and goes inside. Mrs. Bateman is left alone on the porch, staring into space. After a moment, she glances back, making sure she is alone. Then, she turns forward, again.

MRS. BATEMAN
Old house, listen to me. Listen to me, ya hear? You have always been there to me. You have always been tall and sturdy like my
(Cont'd)

MRS. BATEMAN (Cont'd)
prince in shinin' armor. You have always protected me, comforted me, given me strength and courage when I needed it. I need you now. I need you now more than ever.
(sitting forward in the wheelchair)
I am like Joshua at the gates of Jericho. I am ready for battle. But, you've got to give me a sword! I'm dependin' on you! Don't fail me in my darkest hour!
(thrusting her cane in the air))
Give—me—a—*sword*!

The lights fade out. End of Act One.

Act Two

Scene One

Same scene as Act One. Rawley is sitting alone at the table on the porch turning pages in a photo album, there. And he is finding some of the photos amusing. The time is around three p.m., the same day

After a moment, Marge comes out the screen door. She is now wearing jeans, tennis shoes and a light pullover.

MARGE
(spying Rawley)
I wondered where you were.

Rawley only half glances up before going back to the album. Marge then heads toward the front steps, stops, rubbing her arms to warm them up.

MARGE (Cont'd)
Aren't you freezing out here? *(Rawley merely shakes his head)* Well, I am. I forget how cold it gets down here, too. *(looking out at the yard).* This yard just looks terrible. *(glancing over at him)* Am I disturbing you? *(again, Raw;ey shakes his head)* I don't get much of a chance to visit with my darling little brother... What's it like livin' up in New York, now?

RAWLEY
Same...

MARGE
Same as what...?

Rawley laughs out loud at one of the photos.

MARGE (Cont'd)
Same as Paris...? You were over there, I think, weren't you?

                    RAWLEY
            (annoyed with questioning))
Different, Marge. Different than Paris!

                    MARGE
How so…? I'd like to know more about it. I haven't had a chance to go to Paris like you have… and I'm sure Angela has, too. I have been denied all that.

Rawley sighs, continuing with the photos, smiling, again. Marge then approaches him.

                    MARGE
Whachou lookin' at that's so amusin'?

                    RAWLEY
Photos… Marge.

                    MARGE
Photos of what…?

                    RAWLEY
Photos from one of the albums in the living room.

                    MARGE
Well, I'd like to see them, myself. I'm sure I've never even seen them…

                    RAWLEY
              (looking up, finally)
They've been in there our whole lives, Marge! Where have you been?

                    MARGE
I suppose my mother kept them from me like everything else she did.

RAWLEY
Our mother, Marge. And nobody kept anything from you.

MARGE
You are wrong about that, Rawley. You just don't know the half of it. When I was growin' up, I was made to stay out of the house every day. Mother totally ignored me… unlike you… and unlike like *Angela*, of course. She never made *you* stay outside all the time…

RAWLEY
(peeved)
I don't know where you get all that.

MARGE
It's true. I had to play out in the woods by myself. I love my mother but she was never a good mother to *me*.

RAWLEY
(going back to photos)
She was the same mother to all of us, Marge. She was extremely active. She played bridge all the time, went to parties and functions, shot archery with daddy frquently before he died… you just took things personally, is all. Get over it!

MARGE
I can't get over it. That kind of thing affects children for the rest of their lives.

RAWLEY
Whatever.

Rawley then closes the photo album in a huff
.

MARGE
Mind if I sit down with you for a minute?

RAWLEY
Suit yourself. *(gesturing then to album)* Here, look at some of the photos, if you want.

MARGE
(moving to sit down opposite)
Maybe I'll look at them, later. I want to talk to you about somethin' important.

Rawley, sighs, preparing himself for her usual complaints.

MARGE (Cont'd)
It's about our mother…

RAWLEY
That's all been settled, Marge.

MARGE
No, it hasn't.

Rawley sits back, folding him arms and getting ready for more nagging.

MARGE (Cont'd)
I have decided to move back down here… in this house.

RAWLEY
(annoyed)
You know that's not possible, Marge.

MARGE
Why? I can take care of this place while mother's up in Arkadelphia…

RAWLEY
Angela's already told us she's sellin' the house.

                    MARGE
I know she told us that, and it's a shame. I could turn this yard into a beautiful garden.

                    RAWLEY
It's not gonna happen, Marge. Angela will need the money from a sale to pay for mother's expenses where she's goin'.

                    MARGE
Most of that's will go into Angela's pockets, believe you me.

Rawley grabs for the photo album, gets up and heads for the screen door.

                    RAWLEY
I don't wanna discuss it *any* further.

He then goes inside while Marge stares after him. Then, she stands up, glances, disapprovingly, at the yard, again, then heads for the screen door, herself. She jerks it open then enters slamming it shut, as before.

About the same time, Abraham appears, coming from the side of the house, carrying a big fat pumpkin. When he reaches the front, he sits the pumpkin down on the porch edge then steps back to get a full view of it. We see that it is a traditional jack-o'-lantern with a smiling face carved in it, already lit. At that, the screen door opens, again, and Laurie comes out.

                    LAURIE
Afternoon, Abraham.

                    ABRAHAM
Hidy, Miss Laurie.

Laurie then approaches, sitting down at the steps. She notices the jack-o'-lantern, right away, of course.

LAURIE
Oh, how adorable. Did you make that, yourself?

ABRAHAM
Well, Miss Laurie, t'tell y'all the truth, I just went down and gots a pumpkin from Mr. Jameson's store like Miss Bettye done told me to do. Calley, now, in the kitchen… she done carved the face in it.

LAURIE
Well, it looks mighty nice if I do say so, myself.

ABRAHAM
It sho does, Miss Laurie. And I sho hopes Miss Bettye is pleased with it.

LAURIE
Well, it might be a while before we find that out. She's gone and locked herself up in her room. I've tried to get her to open the door but she just won't do it. She tells me to go away whenever I try. I don't know what else to do.

ABRAHAM
Ain't nothin' y'all can do, Miss Laurie. Miss Bettye, she gots a mind of her own. Always has and always will. Ain't nobody gonna tell Miss Bettye what to do.

LAURIE
Nobody 'cept her daughter, I guess.

ABRAHAM
Well, now, that remains to be seen.

Abraham then reaches for his leaf broom against the porch and begins raking up some newly-fallen leaves while talking.

ABRAHAM (Cont'd)
Like I told you, Miss Laurie, I been here a *long* time. And, well, lemme tell y'all somethin'. Whenever things look like they's 'bout t'change... well, things just has a way of staying like theys always been. No what I mean?

LAURIE
I don't know 'bout that, Abraham. This time, it might be different. Miss Bateman has her mind made up about her mother goin' off to that retirement home. And it doesn't look like anybody's gonna change it.

ABRAHAM
Where y'all from, Miss Laurie? Y'all from 'round these parts?

LAURIE
My word, no. I'm from way up in Tennessee.

ABRAHAM
Is that right?! I thought y'all was from 'round here. Sho'nuf could o'fooled me. How in the world did y'all come to be down here?

LAURIE
Well, I'm embarrassed to say. I came down here with my boyfriend and soon as we got here, he dumped me before headin' on out west, somewheres. So, here I am.

ABRAHAM
Well, now, ain't that somethin'. Y'all gots no family a'nothin'?

LAURIE
Nope. I went and got me a job cleanin' houses. But, I just take care of the elderly, now. I like that a lot better.

ABRAHAM
Sho'nuf. Sho'nuf.

Laurie continues observing Abraham raking the leaves.

LAURIE
What was Judge Bateman like, Abraham? I've heard a lot about him. Was he as nice a man as they say he was?

ABRAHAM
(pausing with the raking)
Oh, Miss Laurie, Judge Bateman, he was very nice. He was 'bout the nicest white folk y'all eva did see.

LAURIE
Is *that* right?

ABRAHAM
Sho'nuf. Why, not a Christmas went by that Judge Bateman didn't see that eva poor folk in this here town got somethin' good to eat fo' Christmas dinner.

LAURIE
You mean he'd pay for it out of his own pocket?

ABRAHAM
Well, not like that. Not like that. Y'all see, he was the one who headed up the Christmas food drive, eva year. Y'all know, eva'body donatin' can goods and all that so all the poor folks wouldn't go hungry. He collected toys, too, for the l'il chillins.

LAURIE
I wish I had known him.

ABRAHAM
I wish you had, too, Miss Laurie. He was a very nice man.

LAURIE

Ever wonder how come there are so many good people in this world and so many bad ones, too? I wonder what makes some good and others not?

ABRAHAM

Well, Miss Laurie, ain't nobody all good and ain't nobody all bad. I figure there's good and bad in us all. That's just the way things is.

LAURIE

You are very wise, Abraham. You really are.

ABRAHAM
(chuckling)
I don't know 'bout that, Miss Laurie. Could be. Could be.

Charlene then appears, coming briskly up the walk.

CHARLENE

Abraham!

ABRAHAM
(turning)
Oh, hidy, Miss Charlene.

CHARLENE
(approaching him)
Anything new happenin' since I was over here this mornin'?

ABRAHAM

Well, I cain't rightly say. I been downtown to Mr. Jameson's sto' fo'most o' that time.

CHARLENE

I was just wonderin' how Mrs. Bateman is taking all this.

ABRAHAM
Well, Miss Charlene, she ain't too happy. No, ma'am. She ain't too happy, at all.

CHARLENE
I've been tryin' to reach Franklin all mornin' long, but he's been out in the field. I am just beside myself. And, my mother is just devastated.

ABRAHAM
Yes, Miss Charlene. I knows how y'alls feels. I knows just how y'alls feels.

Charlene then spies Laurie standing up to greet her.

CHARLENE
Laurie!

ABRAHAM
I was just wonderin', Miss Charlene…

CHARLENE
(ignoring him for Laurie)
Anything new happen I should know about?

LAURIE
Mrs. Bateman and her daughter Miss Angela have been havin' words ever since you left here, this mornin'. But, I don't think there's been much of a change. Miss Bateman told me to pack up some of her mother's belongings to take with her to the Good Shepherd Retirement Home, at four. I just haven't been able to bring myself to do it, yet.

CHARLENE
(who has now climbed to the porch)
Well, I suppose Angela's gonna go through with it, after all.

LAURIE
Isn't there anything anybody can do, Mrs. Meeks?

CHARLENE
I wish there were. I have been tryin' to reach my husband ever since he left here at the crack o' dawn, but I have had no luck. He's a salesman, you see, and they are very hard to reach once they leave home. I'm just worried sick.

Abraham climbs the steps while the two women are conversing.

LAURIE
Mrs. Bateman's gone and locked herself up in her room and she's refusin' to answer me whenever I knock. I'm just afraid she might be goin' to try doin' somethin' awful to herself.

CHARLENE
Oh, My Lord. That wouldn't be good. That wouldn't be good, at all.

ABRAHAM
Miss Charlene, I was just wonderin'…

CHARLENE (Cont'd)
(to Laurie)
Where is Angela?

LAURIE
In her room, I guess. She's been up there ever since she and Mrs. Bateman had words, again. I asked her if there was anything I could do to help but she just ignored me.

CHARLENE
Well, she can be like that. She didn't mean it personally, I'm sure.

LAURIE
Oh, no, Mrs. Meeks. I'm sure she didn't. She's just got so much on her mind.

There is commotion, within.

MRS. BATEMAN (OS)
Why is it I have to do everything for myself around here?! Nobody answers me when I call! I might as well be gone from here, already! *Laurie?* Where is that girl? *Laurie! Calley!* Somebody *please* answer me!

LAURIE
Excuse me, Mrs. Meeks. I guess Mrs. Bateman has decided to come out, after all.

Laurie hurries to the screen door, disappearing inside.

CHARLENE
(turning)
Abraham! Did Mrs. Bateman say anything to you that might lead you to believe she might try and do somethin' harmful to herself?

ABRAHAM
Well, now, Miss Charlene, I can't rightly recall 'cept she done told me we was both 'bout to be cooked.

CHARLENE
Cooked!

ABRAHAM
Well, y'all knows how she talks, Miss Charlene. She was meanin' we was both in a heap a trouble, is all.

CHARLENE
(pondering)
I see.

ABRAHAM
I was just wonderin' 'bout somethin'…

Just then, the screen door flies open and Mrs. Bateman comes rolling out having pushed it with her cane. And Laurie is wheeling her out from behind.

MRS. BATEMAN
(to Laurie)
I know I said I didn't want to talk to anyone but I have changed my mind. I've decided I need some fresh air. Wheel me on over to the table, ya hear?

LAURIE
Yes, Mrs. Bateman.

MRS. BATEMAN
(saying hello)
Charlene…

CHARLENE
Hi, Mrs. Bateman. I thought I'd come over this afternoon and see if there was anything I could do to help.

MRS. BATEMAN
You should've brought that shotgun I asked for, earlier.

CHARLENE
(ignoring that)
My mother said to tell you she is very upset about things and she
(Cont'd)

CHERLENE (Cont'd)
thinks it's an outrage what Angela is forcin' on you. And, I do, too. We have all got to put our thinkin' caps on, here, and come up with somethin' to stop it.

LAURIE
Yes, we have to think of somethin'!

ABRAHAM
Well, I was just wonderin'…

CHARLENE
Not now, Abraham. We have to put our minds together on this and come up with somethin' constructive.

ABRAHAM
I know that, but…

CHARLENE
Now, Abraham, this is *very important*!

MRS. BATEMAN
(taking sudden interest)
What is it, Abraham?

ABRAHAM
Well, Miss Bettye, I was wonderin' how come if Judge Bateman done said y'all could live in this house 'till y'all dies, and I could live out back in the shed as long as y'all is up here in the big house, then how come Miss Angela, she can come heres, now, and make y'all do somethin' y'all do not wants t'do?

CHARLENE
We all know Judge Bateman said Mrs. Bateman could live in this house 'til she dies, Abraham, but it was never spelled out in a will.

ABRAHAM
Yes, it was.

CHARLENE
No, it wasn't. There *was* no will. I told you Judge Bateman didn't...

ABRAHAM
Yes, it was.

CHARLENE
Judge Bateman left a trust, Abraham, but he did not leave a will.

ABRAHAM
That is what I been tryin' t'tell y'alls. He sho'nuf did leave a will and I gots a copy of it.

CHARLENE
What in the world do you mean?

ABRAHAM
I been tryin' to tell y'alls... Judge Bateman, he done come to me one day and he said, "Abe," he said, "I want y'all to keep a copy of this here will that says my daughter can live in this house 'till she dies and y'alls can live out back in this here shed so long as she lives, up there." He done give me a copy as proof if eva I needs it, and I still gots my copy.

The three women look at each other, then,

CHARLENE, MRS. BATEMAN AND LAURIE
(in unison)
Where *is* it?!

####### ABRAHAM
I gots it out back in the shed. That is what I been tryin' to tell y'alls. I gots a copy of that will.

####### CHARLENE, MRS. BATEMAN AND LAURIE
####### *(in unison)*
Go *get* it!

####### MRS. BATEMAN
And bring it back here this very minute!

####### ABRAHAM
I sho will. I am gonna git it, right now.

Abraham turns and hurries to the porch end, jumps to the ground and disappears, back.

####### CHARLENE
Well, my *livin'* days!

####### LAURIE
Oh, Mrs. Bateman! Do you think it might really be true?

####### MRS. BATEMAN
I don't know, Laurie, but I'm gonna sure' find out.

####### CHARLENE
And to think he gave a copy to Abraham, of all things!

####### MRS. BATEMAN
More important, if my daddy *did* leave a will, I'd like to know just what happened to it upon his death? I have a sneakin' suspicion there have been some shady dealin's goin' on around here and I intend to get to the bottom of it.

CHARLENE
And you are right to do so, Mrs. Bateman. I don't trust that Mr. Gershwin any furthe' than I can see with both eyes closed.

MRS. BATEMAN
Offerin' to buy my house, my word! A thief is what he is!

CHARLENE
You are right, Mrs. Bateman. He is nothin' but a thief!

Abraham then reappears from the back with the will in hand.

ABRAHAM
Here it is! Here it is! I gots it right here! I gots it right here in my hand!

Abraham hurries to the front and up the steps handing the will out to a waiting Mrs. Bateman who takes and begins scanning it.

MRS. BATEMAN
(summarizing out loud)
'I, Lewis Gilbert Bateman... sound mind... last will and testament... trust... house... daughter Bettye Lynn... in the house... *'til she dies!*'
(lowering will)
Charlene, you have got to do me a very big favor, ya hear?!

CHARLENE
Yes, Mrs. Bateman!

MRS. BATEMAN
You've got to get over to Chestnut Street and find Mr. Rivenbark, this very minute!

CHARLENE
Right!

MRS. BATEMAN

And you've got to tell him this is an emergency! He has got to get over here lickity-split, ya hear?

CHARLENE

Right!

MRS. BATEMAN

I've got to know if this will is valid and I've got to know that, right *now*!

CHARLENE

Right!

MRS. BATEMAN

Go on, now, fast as you can go!

CHARLENE

I certainly will!

Charlene turns and flies off the porch, down the walk and disappears offstage.

MRS. BATEMAN
(to God above)

Lord, my *sword* is at hand!

Just then, the screen door opens and Angela comes out onto the porch. Mrs. Bateman hastily stuffs the will into her side basket, concealing it.

ANGELA

Laurie, have you packed my mother's bag like I asked you to do?

LAURIE

I was just about to do it, Miss Bateman.

ANGELA
There isn't much time. The limo will be here at four.

LAURIE
(glancing at Mrs. Bateman, then back)
Yes, Miss Bateman.

ABRAHAM
Well, I 'specs I better be gittin' on back to my work, then.

Abraham turns and heads to the porch end stepping off and disappearing, back.

ANGELA
(reminding Laurie, again)
Laurie…?

LAURIE
Oh, yes, Miss Bateman. I'm goin' right this instant.

Laurie turns, hesitantly moves to the screen door and opens it. She turns back, though.

LAURIE (Cont'd)
I just wanna say, Miss Bateman, that I think it's a shame what you're doin' to your mother. I think it's a terrible shame.

ANGELA
(chastising her)
Laurie!

LAURIE
I know I shouldn't get involved, but I just feel somebody ought to tell you that to your face. It's a terrible, terrible shame.

ANGELA
I've heard what you have to say. Now, if you don't mind, I'd like to have a word, alone, with my mother.

Laurie is about to break into tears, turns and disappears inside slamming the screen door behind her.

ANGELA (Cont'd)
(staring after her)
That was certainly unexpected...

Angela then turns back to find her mother staring out to the yard.

ANGELA (Cont'd)
I hope you don't intend to make this any more difficult than it already is, mother.

Getting no reply, Angela walks past to the end of the porch and looks out at the trees, again.

ANGELA (Cont'd)
Do you remember when I was little how you used to set the card table up for me in the living room and how you would give me little projects to do? Projects like coloring in my coloring book, and how you would give me a red star if I was good at it and a green star if I was really good? And, if I never crossed a line, if I kept all of the crayons inside the lines of the drawings, I would then get a *gold* star. There weren't very many of those. I was so little and I tried so very hard to be perfect.
(turning back))
I wanted so much to please you, mother. I have always wanted to do that. I have always worked hard for your gold stars. That is why this is particularly painful for me, now.

Angela turns back around, staring out at the trees, again. After a moment,

MRS. BATEMAN

I only wanted you to make the most of your life, Angela. I never meant you any harm. I'm sorry if I hurt you in any way.

ANGELA

Well, what's done is done.
(turning her direction, again)
I wish there were more time to take care of all this but I'm afraid there isn't. I have to be back in L.A., tomorrow. I'm starting a picture in two days and I need time to prepare. I hope you understand.

MRS. BATEMAN

Of course. You're career…

ANGELA
(approaching her)
I haven't told Marge or Rawley much of anything about this.

MRS. BATEMAN

No matter.

ANGELA

I'll ask Mr. Gershwin to put in a call to both of them for me, later. Is there anything you want them to know?

MRS. BATEMAN

About what…?

ANGELA

Well, about any of this? Mr. Gershwin can tell them that when he calls.

MRS. BATEMAN

No… nothing.

ANGELA
So, you'll cooperate, then.

MRS. BATEMAN
As if I have a choice.

ANGELA
Well, you might make things easy... for yourself?

MRS. BATEMAN
I think I'd like some time out here, alone, Angela.

ANGELA
All right. I need to finish packing, anyway.

Angela then walks to the screen door, opening it, then turning back.

ANGELA (Cont'd)
Is there anything you'd like Laurie to bring out to you?

MRS. BATEMAN
(staring outward, again)
No. Not a thing. I just want to be alone.

Angela sighs, then disappears inside. After a moment, Mrs. Bateman takes the will out, again, staring at it, a moment, then clutches it to her bosom. A minute later, Abraham appears peeking around the side of the house. And the screen door opens a crack as Laurie peers cautiously out, as well. A voice offstage is now heard...

CHARLENE (O.S)
And that's when Abraham told us about it. We had no idea it even existed...

Charlene then appears coming up the walk accompanied by MR. RIVENBARK, a short, portly and amiable elderly man wearing a frumpy suit and carrying a weathered leather briefcase, in hand. And he is hurrying to keep up with Charlene's brisk pace.

                CHARLENE (Cont'd)
                  (calling out)
I'm *back*, Mrs. Bateman, and I have Mr. Rivenbark right here with me.

                MRS. BATEMAN
Thank the Lord, Charlene! You are indeed a cherished friend.

As Charlene and Mr. Rivenbark climb the steps to the porch, Laurie slips out the screen door and Abraham comes around to the front, as well.

                MRS. BATEMAN (Cont'd)
I thank you from the bottom of my heart, Mr. Rivenbark, for comin' over here, so quick.

                MR. RIVENBARK
The pleasure is mine, Mrs. Bateman. How very nice to see you, again, after such a long time.

                MRS. BATEMAN
Too long, Mr. Rivenbark. It is, indeed, a pleasure to see you, too.

                CHARLENE
I have been tellin' Mr. Rivenbark about the will.

                MR. RIVENBARK
Yes. Mrs. Meeks has told me you want to know if the will you have is valid, is that correct?

MRS. BATEMAN
That is correct, Mr. Rivenbark. And, here it is.
(displaying the will for him)
I need to know if this is, indeed, my father's last will and testament and if it is a legal and bindin' document.

Mr. Rivenbark then sits his briefcase down and takes out his glasses, slipping them on. He then takes the will from Mrs. Bateman and begins scanning it.

MR. RIVENBARK
Uh-huh… uh-huh… uh-huh… hmm… mm-hmm… huh!

MRS. BATEMAN
Well, is it valid or not?

Mr. Rivenbark then flips the document over and back, again, stares closer at the signatures, once more, then looks directly back at Mrs. Bateman. Laurie and Charlene move in closer and Abraham leans forward from where he is.

MR. RIVENBARK
What you have here, Mrs. Bateman is… well, this happens to be… this happens to be the very will I executed for Judge Bateman, myself. And, it was duly witnessed by my secretary at the time, Mrs. Frances Faye Malone, whose signature is right here at the bottom. And it bears the notary seal, as well, right where it should be.

MRS. BATEMAN
So, Mr. Rivenbark, does that mean it's valid?

MR. RIVENBARK
Not only is it valid, Mrs. Bateman, it is legal and bindin' to the letter.

MRS. BATEMAN
(to God above)
Lead me, Lord, to Jericho!

Screams of delight erupt from both Charlene and Laurie.

ABRAHAM
Halleluiah!

CHARLENE
Does this mean, then, Mrs. Bateman can live in this house 'til she dies, Mr. Rivenbark?

MR. RIVENBARK
That is what the will says, Mrs. Meeks.

CHARLENE
But, her daughter Angela is tryin' to force her into a retirement home, instead. She even told me she'd have her declared incompetent, if necessary.

MR. RIVENBARK
She would have a difficult time tryin' to do a thing like that. No one's gonna declare Mrs. Bateman anything of the sorts. Not while I'm around, I can promise you that.

MRS. BATEMAN
Mr. Rivenbark, you have been away from here *too* long. If you will be so gracious as to accept, I would like to retain you, again, as my lawyer in this matter and in all other legal matters from this moment on.

MR. RIVENBARK
I have always been at your call, Mrs. Bateman. You know that.

MRS. BATEMAN

Yes, I do. It's just that my head has been turned around, here, one too many times, is all. But, I am starin' straight ahead, now. Will you accept?

MR. RIVENBARK

Of course.

To everyone's surprise, Mrs. Bateman steadies herself with her cane and steps right out of her wheelchair onto her own two feet.

LAURIE

Oh, Mrs. Bateman! You can't stand up!

MRS. BATEMAN
(looking around)

Who says I can't?

LAURIE

But...

MRS. BATEMAN

You wanna see me dance?

ABRAHAM

Oh, no, Miss Bettye! Y'all gots to be careful, now!

MRS. BATEMAN

That ol' wheelchair was my daddy's and it served him well. And, it served me well, too. But, I am gettin' my strength back now and I don't think I'll be needin' it, any more. Not while I'm in a fightin' mood!

CHARLENE

Well, isn't that just precious!

Mrs. Bateman then extends a hand to Mr. Rivenbark to seal the deal. Then,

MRS. BATEMAN
Laurie, would you be so kind as to go and tell my daughter Angela she is wanted in the livin' room. Mr. Rivenbark has somethin' very important he needs to discuss with her.

LAURIE
Oh, *yes*, Mrs. Bateman! I'll go and tell her, *right away*!

Laurie hurries to the screen door, disappearing inside.

MRS. BATEMAN
Mr. Rivenbark, you were always a good friend to my daddy Judge Bateman and you have always been a dear friend to me, as well. I am so delighted you are once again here at my house.

MR. RIVENBARK
And I am delighted to be here, again, Mrs. Bateman.

MRS. BATEMAN
If you will be so kind as to meet with my daughter, now, in the livin' room, and explain to her that it is my desire to stay in this house for as long as I choose, just as my daddy willed it, I would be forever grateful to you, sir.

MR. RIVENBARK
Certainly, Mrs. Bateman. The pleasure is mine, as always.

Mr. Rivenbark then moves to the screen door while Charlene hurries to open it for him. He then disappears inside with will in hand and with Charlene following in, afterwards.

MRS. BATEMAN
The walls of Jericho are about to come tumblin' down, Abraham.

ABRAHAM
Halleluiah! Miss Bettye. *Halleluiah!*

Mrs. Bateman then notices the pumpkin sitting on the edge of the porch.

MRS. BATEMAN
Now, that, Abraham, looks like a splendid pumpkin you have brought us!

Abraham hurries to the pumpkin, picks it up and turns its face around so that Mrs. Bateman can see it, fully.

ABRAHAM
Just like y'all wants it, Miss Bettye.

MRS. BATEMAN
Oh, yes! That is a fine jack-o'-lantern if ever I did see. And I believe it has already begun to work its spell. With any luck, the witches won't be gettin' us this year, I reckon.

ABRAHAM
Oh, no, Miss Bettye. Theys is not gonna be gettin' us this year, fo' sho.

MRS. BATEMAN
Put it right back there on the porch's edge so all the little dickens can see it when they come up the walk, tonight.

Abraham then carefully returns the jack-o'-lantern to its noble place, facing outward, again.

ABRAHAM
Sho'nuf, Miss Bettye. Sho'nuf. Just like it has always been.

Angela then comes flying out the screen door with her cell phone, in hand.

ANGELA

Mother, what is this all about... this supposed will of granddaddy's that you are claiming has miraculously turned up out of nowhere? Am I to believe...

Marge and Rawley hurry out, afterwards, with Laurie following.

MRS. BATEMAN

Well, apparently, my daddy *did* leave a will, after all, Angela.

ANGELA

You know as well as I that that's absolutely ridiculous! Don't you think Mr. Gershwin would have known about that, before now?

MRS. BATEMAN

I would've thought so.

ANGELA

Well, then, it's obviously a fake.

MRS. BATEMAN

I'm not so sure about that. Not according to Mr. Rivenbark, it isn't. It is a valid and enforceable document.

ANGELA

This is not going to change a thing at this point, mother. Don't you understand, I cannot deal with you, here, and take care of my career in Hollywood at the same time? It's not as easy for me as it used to be. I am fighting for my professional existence! Don't you understand that? I simply don't have the time nor the energy to take care of both!

MRS. BATEMAN
I am sorry to impose on your career, Angela. My life is so meaningless in comparison to yours, isn't it?

ANGELA
That is not what I meant and you know it.

Mr. Rivenbark then comes out the screen door, again, with the will still in hand.

MR. RIVENBARK
I've just been on the phone with Mr. Gershwin, Miss Bateman. I've told him about the will, in detail.

ANGELA
(turning)
And what did he have to say about it?

MR. RIVENBARK
He would like to discuss that with you, directly. He is waiting for you to call.

ANGELA
I see! Well, with all due respect to you, Mr. Rivenbark, Mr. Gershwin is our *lawyer*…

MRS. BATEMAN
Not *mine*!

ANGELA
And, as trustee of our family estate, I believe I have my rights.

MR. RIVENBARK
As trustee of your *mother's* estate, Miss Bateman, you *do* have your rights. But, at any time Mrs. Bateman should decide to
(Cont's)

MR. RIVENBARK (Cont'd)
remove you as trustee and name some other party trustee in your place, that is also her right. Will or no will, she has that right.

MRS. BATEMAN
(amazed)
I *do*?! No one has ever told me that! I might as well be a lump on a log!

Mr. Riverbark then hands the will back to Mrs. Bateman.

ANGELA
Well, we're going to get to the bottom of this, right this minute.

Angela hastily punches the keys on her cell phone dialing a number. After a moment,

ANGELA
(turning aside, into phone)
Angela Bateman calling. *(brief pause)* Of *course*, for Mr. Gershwin, who else? *(another pause)* Mr. Gershwin, I understand you've spoken with Mr. Rivenbark, here, about… yes… yes… I know all about the will. He showed it to me a few minutes ago. What I want to know is… I know that, but… I know, but… *(pause)* I see. But, that is not what you and I discussed. *(pause)* I see. And that's all you have to say about it? *(pause)* Well, I guess there isn't any reason for my being, here, now, is there? *(pause)* No, there isn't anything else I need from you. *(curtly)* Thank you.

Angela then punches off. After a moment, she turns around.

ANGELA (Cont'd)
Well, mother, apparently Mr. Gershwin concurs with Mr. Rivenbark's assessment of the will. And, to think there was a will all along and none of us even knew about it.

MRS. BATEMAN
(still suspicious)
Yes. Isn't that a right curious thing?

Mrs. Bateman then folds the will and slips it into her sleeve.

ANGELA
So, I guess you'll be staying here in the house, after all.

MRS. BATEMAN
That is my desire. I will also be naming Mr. Rivenbark trustee of my estate from this moment on. I hope you understand.

ANGELA
Well, maybe it's all for the best.

MRS. BATEMAN
Considering how demanding your career is…

ANGELA
Yes, it *is* demanding. (*sighing, then*) Abraham, would you mind helping me with my suitcase in the hallway.

ABRAHAM
Sho'nuf, Miss Angela. *Sho-nuff*! I would be *happy* to. Yes, ma'am. I would be *very happy* to do just that.

Abraham then hurries up the steps to the porch, disappearing inside.

ANGELA
The limo should be here any minute.

                    MRS. BATEMAN
                     (gesturing)
Oh, it's already here. I see it down there at the curb waitin' for
you.

                       ANGELA
                  (seeing it, as well)
So, it is. Well, I've got to be going, then. It's a long way to the
airport from here. I'll just get my purse.

*Angela heads for the screen door, opening it, herself, and going in
while Marge and Rawley clamor in, after her.*

                        MARGE
                    (calling to her)
Does this mean you're not selling the house, Angela?

                    MRS. BATEMAN
                  (to Mr. Rivenbark)
I can't say I'm sorry to see them all leave, Mr. Riverbark.
Sometimes my children just become a thorn in my side.

*The screen door opens, again, and Angela returns with purse in
hand. She is followed by Abraham who is carrying her suitcase.
Abraham then continues on down the steps and walk to offstage.
After another sigh, Angela approaches her mother and dutiful
pecks a kiss on her cheek. Mrs. Bateman is conflicted by it.*

                       ANGELA
Good-bye, mother.

Angela then turns
.
                   ANGELA (Cont'd)
Charlene, will you walk me to the car?

CHARLENE
Of course, hun. I was on my way back home, anyway.

Charlene then takes Angela by the arm and the two descend the steps to the walk. Mrs. Bateman then moves to the porch edge.

MRS. BATEMAN
(calling)
Angela…?

Angela and Charlene stop, mid-walk, although Angela does not turn back.

ANGELA
Yes, mother?

MRS. BATEMAN
You think I could come out to Hollywood for a visit?

ANGELA
(stunned)
Wha…?

MRS. BATEMAN
You think I could come out to visit you, sometime, in Los Angeles?

ANGELA
Oh, mother… *(turning back to her)* I would *love* that…

MRS. BATEMAN
'Course, I haven't been on a plane in ten years, not since I flew over to visit Aunt Monnie in Charleston. I don't suppose they've changed all that much, though. Just bigger, is all… and faster.

ANGELA
You'll do just fine, I'm sure.

MRS. BATEMAN
I know how busy you are and I'd wait for you to have plenty of time before goin'.

ANGELA
I'll make time, mother. Whenever you want to come is all right with me.

MRS. BATEMAN
Well, we'll see...

CHARLENE
Now, that is right precious, if ever I heard.

Angela turns forward, again, and the two girlfriends continue on down the walk, offstage.

MRS. BATEMAN
(calling, again)
Charlene, you tell your mother Bettye Lynn'll be over to visit her, tomorrow, ya hear?

CHARLENE (OS)
(calling back)
I surely *will*, Mrs. Bateman! She'll just be tickled t'death!

MRS. BATEMAN
Mr. Rivenbark, do you like sweet potatoes?

MR. RIVENBARK
I do, Mrs. Bateman.

MRS. BATEMAN

Well, we are havin' them for supper, tonight, and I'd be very pleased if you would stay and have some with us.

MR. RIVENBARK

Thank you, Mrs. Bateman. I would like that.

MR. BATEMAN

Laurie, would you be so kind as to show Mr. Rivenbark into the livin' room, again? And, would you also be so kind as to tell Calley to set another place for Mr. Rivenbark at the dinner table, for us?

LAURIE

I surely will, Mrs. Bateman.

Laurie then goes to the screen door, opening it for Mr. Rivenbark. Mr. Rivenbark then picks up his briefcase and goes on inside with Laurie following in, afterwards.

Mrs. Bateman is now left, alone, on the porch, again. She then looks up at the trees, reflecting. After a moment,

MRS. BATEMAN

Well, old house, you have come to my aide, again, and I thank you. I thank you from the bottom of my heart. You are, indeed, my dearest and closest friend. Thank you. Oh, yes… I thank you.

She then turns and, aided by her trusted cane, moves to the screen door, opens it and disappears quietly inside.

The lights slowly fade to an evening blue with the smiling face of the jack-o'-lantern now glowing a vibrant orange. It continues staring mischievously out at us for a moment, then blackout.

The End

Southern Exposure

Synopsis

<u>Angela</u> <u>Bateman</u>, Hollywood film and TV star whose career has seen better days, returns home to the Deep South to put her mother <u>Bettye</u> <u>Lynn</u> <u>Bateman</u> into a retirement home. Bettye Lynn, who has lived in her Greek revival home since birth, is stunned by the sudden revelation and is, to say the least, in hapless disbelief. The news also troubles next door neighbor Charlene, a childhood friend of Angela, Bettye Lynn's oversensitive caregiver Laurie and her devoted black caretaker Abraham who has been in service to Bettye Lynn since his long-ago traumatic return home from the war. Also arriving for the family debacle are Betty Lynn's two other children Marge, who is intent on taking over as her mother's guardian in spite of woman's horror of that, and Rawley, Betty Lynn's only son and favorite who would prefer to stay out of this family squabble, altogether. Although Bettye Lynn attempts to thwart Angela's intentions as best she can, and her allies surrounding her protest vehemently on her behalf, Angela, who is overwhelmed trying to save her faltering Hollywood career, and who has no time to deal with the frequent problems her mother causes the estate's attorney, proceeds in full force to accomplish her agenda. Confrontations abound and, when all seems a complete loss and the limo is due to arrive any minute to take Betty Lynn away, the one least expected among them rises to the occasion, and Betty Lynn's tragic fate takes on a totally different perspective.

All Rights Reserved

Royalty Guidelines

royalty free for no cost admissions and $20 for licensed nonprofits per performance

royalty for paid admissions: $50 per performance

royalty for paid off-Broadway admissions: $50 per performance

royalty for paid Broadway admissions: negotiated with the author or author's representative

all foreign theatrical performances: follow above guidelines

Contact:
bricbookspublishing@gmail.com

Made in the USA
Middletown, DE
03 October 2022